Flora Flowerdew and the Mystery of the Purloined Papers

FLORA FLOWERDEW VICTORIAN MYSTERIES
BOOK TWO

AMANDA MCCABE

CLOVERLEAF BOOKS

PUBLISHER'S NOTE: This is a work of fiction. Names, characters,
places, and incidents either are the product of the author's
imagination or are used fictitiously. Any resemblance to actual
persons, living or dead, business establishments, events, or locales is
entirely coincidental.

Flora Flowerdew and the Mystery of the Purloined Papers Copyright
2023 © Amanda McCabe

Published by Oliver-Heber Books

0 9 8 7 6 5 4 3 2 1

One

1889

"Cor blimey, Mary, but I'm tired of ghosties and goblins at seances," Flora Flowerdew, nee Florrie Gubbins, cried as her maid, friend, and conspirator Mary helped her out of her heavy "Madame Flowerdew" gown, all black and purple velvet crusted with jet. "They're making me ache and creak more than trotting across the stage ever did."

"Worse'n the stage?" Mary laughed. She'd worked backstage at the Follies longer than Flora had danced in the footlights, and Flora knew she'd seen it all, there amid the racks of spangled tulle, the musty fug of sweat and greasepaint and cheap perfume. Seen love affairs gone right and wrong, rivalries, pranks, even stabbings and pistol-brandishings. It was true, then; séances were easier. At least they didn't last as long. Paid better, too, and her disguise protected her from most men's pawings.

Flora sighed and shook her head with relief as Mary lifted away the black wig pinned with gossamer veils, and cool air rushed through Flora's own red curls. She took out all the tight pins and shook her hair all free over her shoulders. It always took a while to shed that ridiculous Madame Flowerdew and spin back into herself. To feel like Flora, ex-actress and hardworking

1

medium, young(ish) and spending her time reading penny dreadfuls where everything came out well in the end. Unlike life.

"You're right, maybe not *harder* than hoofing it at the Follies," she said. She drew on a pink-flowered silk dressing gown, soft and loose after hours of being weighed down by beads and lace, and sat down at her dressing table to reach for her silver-backed hairbrush. "At least most of the people who come here looking for Grandmama's lost brooch or beg forgiveness from old Papa don't grab at me backside or corner me under the table."

They just sobbed and pleaded, and sometimes got red-faced with anger when their answers didn't come. But that was people for you, always needing to know *everything*. Flora knew sometimes ignorance was just bliss.

Mary brushed at the black gown before she hung it away in the wardrobe, and smoothed the wig on its stand. Madame Flowerdew was expensive to maintain. "But look how busy we are lately! Tonight made four séances this week. Plenty of good beef for the stewpot."

Flora nodded. That was true enough. The séance slots were filled up in the last few months. The pantry was full, the bookstore and milliners made weekly (even twice weekly!) deliveries now. Chou-Chou had a new cushion, striped satin with gold fringe, where she reclined now, cleaning her paws after a long evening of being the most clairvoyant Pomeranian in London. Being known to have helped a *duke* with one's "enormous psychic gifts" would do that in a town impressed with aristocratic associations. Only a royal warrant above her door could help more.

Especially when that aristocrat was a tall, Viking-esque, golden-haired, unmarried (!) duke, in possession of a vast, ancient, though rather rundown estate. The whispers of "Madame Flowerdew was consulted by the

Duke of Everton, who recommends her gifts most highly" brought flocks of patrons to the door.

Flora's hand faltered as she dragged the brush through her red hair. *Benedict*. Just thinking his name made a knot curl up in her stomach. A tight ball of happy memories, longing for what couldn't be.

It had been so long since she saw him. He'd been as busy as her, in his own duke-ly way. Doing work on his estate, coming to London to visit balls and teas and garden parties where young debs gathered, looking for husbands. Being seen at the opera. She read about it all in the Society papers.

Ever since his almost-betrothal to Miss Petrie broke off and she married a vicar instead, Benedict had to find a new heiress to wed. His estate and everyone who worked on it relied on that, after his grandparents lost the fortune that should have maintained his farms and roofs. Surely he could have been married ten times by now, considering all the ladies who dashed about after him! Lady Emerson, Miss Merton, widows and debs and girls whose fathers were rich merchants from the North. Yet Flora hadn't read about an engagement yet. She dreaded it, really, even as it was inevitable.

A duke had to eat and keep a roof over his head, just the same as a spirit medium on her own in the world. Benedict's lack of family fortune and vast land holdings was what brought him (or rather, his deceased and very cranky grandfather) to Madame Flowerdew's door in the first place. That was how the world worked. Even a ghost knew his grandson had to marry a Miss Petrie.

But sometimes, at night when Madame Flowerdew's wig and white face paint were put away and quiet descended over Flora's cozy little flat, she closed her eyes and remembered their adventures last year. The flowers and sunshine of the South of France; the crashing, cold waves and cliffs of Cornwall. She'd never seen such sights, never felt that thrill before! An orphan who

3

moved from factories to stages to séance tables, always scraping and dragging herself up by her fingernails, didn't have time to explore the world out there. But she'd done it with Benedict to share it. And with him beside her, even the blue French sky seemed more vivid, more immediate.

She dropped her brush to the cluttered, lace-draped table with a sharp "crack." Crystal pots and bottle rattled. Mary glanced up from folding black veils, and Chou Chou paused in her ablutions with one paw in the air.

"Sorry," Flora murmured, reaching for the brush again. "Maybe I should retire. Let Madame Flowerdew take her spirit shingle down."

Mary's mouth dropped open for an instant. "Retire? What would we—you do?"

Flora tapped her finger against a perfume bottle, suddenly befuddled. What *would* she do? There was enough saved now that she, Mary, and Chou Chou would be fine, if they were careful. They could move from the Kensington flat, where Florrie Gubbins had so long dreamed of living. Take on a new challenge. Or—what?

She had no idea. Before seeing more of the world with Benedict, leaving Madame Flowerdew behind would never have occurred to her. She'd worked so hard to land at her séance table! Learned all the ghostly tricks, tappings and ectoplasm and cold touches and voices. Who would have known that Chou Chou, rescued from behind a rubbish tip, would be able to discern *real* spirits? And that this would bring a duke to her door?

"I don't know what we would do, really," she said. "Move to the country and keep bees? Grow marrows that win village fetes? Knit?"

Mary snorted. "You've never dug in the dirt or picked up a needle in your life!"

Flora scowled at her. "I could learn! Just like I

4

learned to dance and sing, and summon ghosts. Or maybe I could write. I read enough penny dreadfuls, I could pen a tale of stormy nights at old castles. Or even some silver fork novels! Those are popular, and we've seen enough toffs come through our door. Those books make a tidy sum, I hear."

"I'm sure you could do that, better than that Mrs. Gore everyone loves so much," Mary said soothingly. "I'm just not sure you'd be happy in some country cottage. All that fresh air and quiet, no theaters and shops."

Flora sighed. "I've never tried it, so how would I know? We've been doing this Madame Flowerdew gig for so long, surely there's *something* else out there."

Mary gently patted her shoulder and started to plait Flora's hair. They'd been friends so long, seen so much together, no one could help like Mary could. "You're just tired out, and who can blame you? It's been endless people knocking on our door for weeks now, wanting to talk to their ghosties. Takes it out of you."

Flora nodded. There had indeed been many clients, and she managed to give them what they wanted even though no real spirits had shown up since that late duke and his dratted diamonds. "I am a bit tired. And maybe bored."

Mary nodded. "We could turn them away, go off to the seaside for a bit. Some bathing, walking, time to read, it would set you up nicely."

Chou Chou glanced up, her ears swiveling with interest. Maybe she envisioned prancing down a pleasure pier in her best pink bows, everyone cooing over her beauty.

Flora thought of the pebbled beaches at Cornwall, the dramatic green-gray waves and ruined castles. She knew that wasn't quite the seaside Mary pictured, Brighton or Bath with their tea rooms and candy floss and assemblies. But a change of scene could be good.

"I'll think about it," she said, straightening the bottles that had gone awry.

Mary nodded, and tied off the end of the plait. "In the meantime, you just get some sleep and forget about the appointment book. I'll go make you some of my special cocoa..."

A sudden knock at the front door shattered the peaceful boredom of the night. Flora started up from her chair, her heart pounding. The little porcelain-flowered clock on the fireplace mantel said it was past midnight. Even the most desperate spirit-seeker never called so late. Surely a visit at this hour meant only one thing —trouble.

Flora and Mary exchanged a long glance, until another knock sounded. They both reached for daggers designed as ivory-handled letter openers on the bedside table. Chou Chou went very still, the caramel-colored ruff of fur at her neck bristling.

"I'll just go see who that is, then," Mary said, and smoothed the white apron over her black parlor-maid dress.

As she swept out of the room, Flora slowly stood up and tightened the sash of her dressing gown around her. She listened closely to Mary move through the flat, the click of the door, a murmur of voices. A cry of happiness.

Mary came rushing back in, smiling now, her eyes bright. "It's Benedict! Er, His Grace, the Duke of Everton. And a lady who says she's his aunt."

Benedict was there! Flora clapped with delight, her stomach nervously-happily flip-flopping. He had come back! But why now, so late at night? Was his grandfather back again?

Hmm. It was true. Trouble had come back indeed. And she just had to hope it was the good sort.

6

Two

When Flora stepped into her sitting room, (her own private sitting room, not the grand and gloomy séance chamber), she had to stop herself from rushing to Benedict and kissing his handsome cheek. He looked just the same as he had when they were dashing around France and Cornwall together, tall, broad-shouldered in his black evening jacket and cream brocade waistcoat, golden of hair and skin, green eyes like emeralds. Yet there was a new wariness in those eyes, a strange distance in his smile. She froze in the doorway. "Benedict. How nice to see you again."

"Flora," he answered, sounding uncertain, just as she felt. "I'm sorry to call so late."

Chou Chou didn't care about nuances. She pranced right up to him, twirling around on her back legs with her front paws waving in the air as she yipped merrily. Benedict scooped her up and tossed her in the air before kissing the top of her fluffy little head, and the Benedict who had become their friend, laughing and happy and kind, was there again.

"What an adorable puppy," the lady next to him said. "Ever so much more appealing than my sister's dreadful Pekingese!"

Flora glanced at her. Like Benedict, she was tall, but very slender in a fashionable evening gown and short cloak of marigold-colored cut velvet. Her silver hair was swept high and crowned with yellow and cream feathers, and topaz and diamonds glinted at her throat and ears. It was clear she had once been a great beauty, with lavender eyes under delicately arched brows and high cheekbones, and she was still lovely.

"How do you do..." Flora began.

"This is my aunt, or great-aunt really. Imogen, Lady Hastings, my grandmother's sister," Benedict said. "Most call her Lady Imogen, she and Grandmama were daughters of an earl."

"But please do not think I am the least like the dowager duchess," Lady Imogen declared with a shudder. "We haven't spoken in years. I'm far too naughty for her approval. Thankfully."

Flora found she rather liked this Lady Imogen, with that gleam in her gorgeous eyes that did indeed seem "naughty." She wouldn't be full of stories of ruling the Empire like the dowager duchess had been. "I'm too naughty for most folks, I should think, so I fully understand."

Lady Imogen gave a crack of laughter. "Indeed! I did know you would be exactly the one to help us. Didn't I say so, Benedict?"

Benedict gave Flora a rueful smile. "You did. But I am sorry for calling so late, truly, Flora. Aunt Imogen insisted."

Flora nodded. She doubted his aunt could ever be thwarted.

"It is my very naughtiness that brought us here, I'm afraid," Lady Imogen said. She didn't really sound apologetic in the least. "It's rather gotten us into a tangle, you see."

Flora nodded again. She'd been right. Trouble. "I am all ears. Do come in, Benedict, Lady Imogen. Shall we have some tea?" She gestured to a cozy grouping of tapestry-upholstered armchairs and hassocks by the carved wood fireplace.

"If you will call me just Imogen, my dear. I'm beyond weary of always being reminded of my father, or worse my old husband the late Lord Hastings. May his foolish old heart rest in peace far from me!" So it seemed she had not come seeking her husband. She led the way to the chairs, settling herself in one as Chou Chou clambered up into her lap. Flora and Benedict sat across from her, scooting their chairs closer across the faded, flowered carpet.

"I'll just fetch some refreshments," Mary said, and rushed out so she wouldn't miss anything.

Benedict leaned closer to Flora, and she sighed at the woodsy, lemony, sunshine scent of his delicious cologne. "I really am sorry," he whispered. "I did try to stop Aunt Imogen from rushing over here so late after Lady Alstruther's ball, but once she has an idea in her head she won't be stopped."

Flora laughed, trying to look anywhere but into those emerald eyes of his. "I can certainly imagine. But never you worry, dukie—I was just whining to Mary that things have become boring here lately. I even said we'd move to the country, and knit and keep bees!"

"Never!" Benedict said, with that dark, chocolate-y laugh of his. It had been too long since she'd heard it. "I just can't picture it, Flora, you and Chou Chou and Mary tending your rhododendrons and chairing church fetes."

"Well, boredom can make a person desperate, you know." Or maybe he didn't, he'd been so busy in the Society pages lately. "Or probably you don't. So much to do for dukes!"

"London *is* dull after Cornwall." He smiled down at her. "It's good to see you again, Flora."

"Good to see you, too, dukie."

"You might not think so after you talk to Aunt Imogen."

Lady Imogen let out a loud "harrumph," and Flora spun around to find her watching Benedict and Flora with a little frown. "If you are quite done apologizing for me and my late hours, Benedict, I should like to speak to the lady."

"Of course, Aunt Imogen," Benedict said, sitting straight up like a chastened schoolboy. Mary hurried in, arranging tea, cakes, and a bottle of Flora's best claret on the low, marble-topped table, along with a bowl of biscuits for Chou Chou.

"Now, Miss Flowerdew..." Lady Imogen began.

"Flora," Flora insisted. She gestured at the dog ensconced on Lady Imogen's velvet and satin lap. "And that is Chou Chou."

"Ah, yes, the gifted Mademoiselle Chou Chou." Imogen patted Chou Chou's fuzzy head. "Well, Flora, I must beg for your assistance. Benedict told me all about your search for those wretched diamonds, and I am in need of just such persistent and creative help. A most unfortunate matter has arisen."

"Unfortunate?" Flora's hand paused for an instant as she poured the tea, but her stage training proved its worth yet again and she just kept smiling politely. She'd been right—trouble. Was that bright, quick flutter deep inside wary, trepidation—or excited?

Imogen took a pink-iced cake and tasted it with a happy sigh before her frown returned. "Yes. You see, my dear, you might not think it to look at my withered old bones now, but I was once quite the vision and much sought after! Every artist wanted to paint my portrait, every poet wrote odes to my eyes and my golden hair. I nearly eloped with the King of Westaria, and then a Russian grand duke, before good sense prevailed and I struck, mostly, to English admirers." She sighed. "Yes, I was quite the fashion back then."

"I would imagine that has not changed much," Flora said truthfully. Imogen was indeed still exceedingly lovely, and obviously passionate. And Flora did remember hearing gossip of the legendary Lady Hastings, which she now recalled since the woman sat right before her. Everyone had once been in love with her. It must have rather embarrassed the straight-laced dowager duchess to have such a sister!

"You are kind indeed." Imogen fed Chou Chou a cake, and gestured for a glass of wine. "I married so I was very silly and had no idea what to do. How to make something of my life. My older sister Violet—you have met her, yes?"

Flora remembered the dowager duchess in her grand French drawing room, talking of the days she and her husband ruled India. "Indeed."

"Then you know. She bossed me terribly when we were in the schoolroom, and by the time I made my debut, she was a duchess. She still tried to direct me, but I would have none of it. I wanted my own pathway, though I had no idea what that would be."

"I understand completely," Flora murmured. She, too, had been pushed and pulled by people all her life, and had struggled to break free.

Imogen gave her a small, sad smile. "I thought you might. I was quite fortunate, really. I met Lord Hastings, much older than myself, of course, but such a dear. He wanted someone to run an elegant home for him, which I certainly did, and maybe provide and heir, which sadly I could not. Beyond that, he wanted only for me to be happy. He died after a few years, and left me a fortune. Then I met Lord Margrave."

"The Earl of Margrave?" Flora asked, thinking of tales she'd heard of the man, who had been a legend in politics in his time, once mooted to be Prime Minister, though it had not come to pass. He'd been famously handsome, too, with a wife who was a duke's daughter.

"Yes, I am sure you have heard of him. A great man, great indeed." Imogen's lavender eyes shimmered over the edge of her wineglass. "What a gorgeous specimen of manhood he was! And so brilliant. The country lost a great deal when he was not made Prime Minister." She laughed roughly, as if half in tears at memories. "He taught me so much, both in the bedchamber and out of it. He had this thing he did with his tongue, you see..."

"Aunt Imogen!" Benedict cried.

Flora gaped at her. She'd certainly heard and seen much in her days, but not a lady talking about an earl's tongue right in front of her nephew. "He was your lover, then?"

"Oh, yes, though not for as long as I would have liked. He was so busy, the poor darling, not much time for fun, and I had many admirers by then. But we stayed good friends, and I learned much from him. Politics, art, history."

"Is this about Lord Margrave, then?" Flora asked, remembering recently reading of the man's death in the newspapers. "You want to talk to his ghost? Make sure he doesn't talk of all you, er, learned together?"

Imogen waved this away with a flash of her bejeweled fingers. "No, not really. He has been dead for months, and he was always the soul of discretion. Usually. He did write me some fascinatingly frank letters."

"So, it's letters you want back from him?" Flora asked, confused. "Letters causing you to worry?"

"Oh, yes. He was a wonderful man, and usually quite wise, but not always as careful about putting his thoughts to paper, when he trusted someone as we trusted each other. And I was foolish enough to keep them. I recently had a little soiree in my townhouse, you see, to remember dear Margrave, and invited many of his family and old friends. I really should not have. That was when they were stolen. Right from my library safe!" For the first time, she seemed to crack a bit, and a sob escaped. Benedict reached over to take her hand, and Chou Chou gave a little lick to her cheek.

Flora thought all this over. Stolen letters. People did sometimes want to know where objects went after someone died, where things had been hidden, questions for spirits. Not usually about thefts *after* their demise, though. "When were these letters written?"

Imogen dabbed at her eyes and took another sip of wine. "They are not new, of course. Around 1859, I should think. Yet I could not bear to part with them over the years. They are of a most *intimate* and *sensitive* nature. Not just of a sexual nature, but also concerning a great scandal of that year, which encompassed even the queen."

Flora sat back in her chair, thinking over all of that information. If word got out about a scandal involving royalty, even so long after the fact, it could be embarrassing, but vital?

Mary eyed the low level in the wine bottle. "Should I fetch the whiskey?"

"Yes, thank you, Mary," Flora said. "I think it's time."

Imogen nodded. "These letters, I fear, could be a revival of scandal. Most embarrassing. Not for me, you understand—I am too old for such worries. But for people I care about very much, including Benedict."

Flora glanced at Benedict, who looked puzzled. "What was in these letters?"

Imogen hesitated, but Benedict squeezed her hand. "I told you, Aunt Imogen. Flora is absolutely to be relied upon."

Chou Chou tapped her velvet sleeve with one amber-furred paw, as if to add reassurances.

Imogen finally nodded, and after a deep gulp of Flora's best whiskey said, "I am sure you can imagine much of it. Some of it rather silly, I'm afraid, young love being what it is, and some truly nonsensical nicknames. He was such a virile man! So vital. And a great deal of his confidences in me, as I had some of both sides of our correspondence. Margrave returned some of my letters when he became ill."

"I can see where that might wag some tongues, as I hear Lord Margrave is to be buried soon in Westminster Abbey with all honors," Flora said. 'But surely it's nothing new, there must be more gossip to replace it."

Imogen smiled wryly. "So old tittle-tattle won't matter? I would certainly agree with you, but in this case there is something rather more monumental involved. Margrave's son, Peter, has been following in his father's political footsteps, and is soon to be granted a very high office in the Cabinet. A place of great trust and prestige. He has been working for this so very long, and his father would be so proud. The country *needs* his good service! He has had some kerfuffle about his marriage lately, but I am sure that will all work out soon enough, and there can be not another stain of doubt about him. Some of Margrave's letters talk of the scandal of 1859, and I fear he was more involved in that little sordid matter than anyone knew. Or *can* know."

"Surely the current Lord Margrave can only have been a child back then!" Mary said.

"But you see, my dears, that is the least of it," Imogen answered. "Peter is known as my godson, but he is actually my own son. He was born in the country, and given to Margrave and his wife to raise. If word of his true parentage emerged..."

Flora couldn't hold back a gasp. An earl was actually illegitimate! And the look on Imogen's face, so sad, so worried, was rather heart-rending. It was obvious she cared greatly for Peter. Even Chou Chou looked taken aback, and Benedict gaped at his aunt.

"You never said," he told her, and Imogen shook her head.

"How could I? I didn't want to let him go back

then, but I was a new widow, no one to hide behind by then. Margrave and his wife, a saintly creature of great earnestness and very high birth, had only two daughters and was ill. They took Peter as their son, and now he is the earl. I'm only his doting godmother, even he believes that. He can know nothing about this! And I will protect him and his career with every ounce of strength I have left. I just need help now. I beg you, Flora..."

Flora could only nod, her throat ached with tears for the old lady. She had no child herself, but she understood that protectiveness, that helpless feeling. "You say they were taken from a gathering at your home. Do you suspect anyone in particular?"

Imogen took another long drink of whiskey, her expression thoughtful. Mary took out a notebook and pencil from one of the table's drawers to make notes.

"Too many, I fear, and they were all at my home that evening. The library where the safe is kept was unlocked, though clearly someone discovered the combination and forced it open." She tapped her emerald-decked finger on her chin. "There was old Margrave's nephew, Roger. A good enough man, I always thought, though quite dull. He has a pretty estate, but not much money. He would have been the heir if not for Peter. And Roger's wife Adele. She is the daughter of Sir Anthony Paddington, another of my long-ago amours, though that liaison was short-lived. I know Adele is most ambitious, and always has been. She reminds me of my sister. Heaven knows why she married Roger. If she found out she could be a countess..."

"Would they be smart enough to get the safe open?" Flora asked.

"Anyone could, I suppose. I am careful about who knows the combination, but servants can be bribed." Imogen thought again for a moment. "There is the neighbor of Margrave's estate, Thomas, Lord Windermere, of Windermere Abbey. He has two daughters, including Belle, who is married to Peter, though I think they seldom live together now. Such a sad estrangement, but many couples do live rather separate lives. Belle does not seem content with the situation as it is. Peter has a lover, you see, Mrs. Jane Annis, a great beauty."

"Would Belle be looking for an excuse to divorce, maybe?" Flora asked. "Or ask her father for help?"

"Possibly. Belle has always been an unhappy sort, despite her advantages. And Thomas might once have had a tendre for Jane himself." Imogen patted Chou Chou as she thought. "Thomas's other daughter is Marianne, a lovely, intelligent girl, if a bit quiet. We all have hopes for her and Benedict to make a match, since things did not work out with the Petrie girl. Marianne has such a fine dowry."

"She is to marry Benedict?" Flora cried in surprise. She glanced at Benedict, who smiled wryly.

"He must marry well, of course, and Marianne Windermere would do nicely. So I cannot allow a scandal to affect this match, too," Imogen said.

"Would Lord Windermere help one daughter gain a divorce if it casts doubts on his other daughter's chance to marry a duke?" Mary asked.

"Very good question, my dear. Lord Windermere is an odd sort, one can never tell what he's thinking. Most unusual, for most men will tell you anything at all at any moment, thinking everyone must find it fascinating." Imogen reached for her beaded reticule, and took out an engraved card. "Luckily, I have procured an invitation to a house party at Windermere Abbey, where everyone I mentioned will be in attendance! We can all go, and make a thorough search. Flora, you can pretend to be my companion. I have heard of your fine dramatic skills."

Flora nodded, feeling that spark of excitement again. To play a part, to find the truth—her boredom vanished. "If you think it would be of help."

"Assuredly! We must make sure everyone I care about is safe from my own youthful follies." She patted Chou Chou again. "I also thought perhaps we could have one tiny séance, ask dear Margrave himself if he has any idea of where to search. It is so hard to know where to begin!"

"We can do it before the party," Flora said, and Chou Chou squeezed her eyes shut in agreement. "I am sure between us all we can find out where the letters are, if they are not yet destroyed."

Imogen smiled brilliantly, and Flora could easily see why every gentleman in London had once been her admirer. "I knew you could help us!" She held up her half-full glass. "To our success!"

Three

It was very early the next morning when Flora left the flat to catch an omnibus top her friend Evie's newspaper office in Fleet Street, much earlier than she usually started the day. Nothing worthwhile ever seemed to happen before noon, but today she saw crowds of dark-suited, bowler-hatted men heading to their offices, nannies with their charges in prams headed to the parks, shops opening their shutters.

Despite the unholy early hour, she couldn't help a little bounce in the step of her buttoned kid boots. She had a new walking dress, purple and white striped with a cunning little jacket *a la militaire*, the bright colors she always preferred to Madame Flowerdew's blacks, and a new hat in the latest style, tip-tilted and feathered. Its ribbon trim fluttered in the cool breeze. Mary had expertly curled and braided her red hair, and it peeked from beneath the satin brim in what she thought was a rather fetching way. If Benedict was getting married, as he had to, she had to forget him and remember she was a pretty enough woman anyway!

She always felt much better when she could toss off that Madame Flowerdew get-up, leaving black wigs and veils in the wardrobe and step outside as a young(ish), fashionable mademoiselle for a while. No one asking her to read their tarot cards or hunt down ghosts—except for Lady Imogen, which was what brought Flora out that day anyway. She was just Flora for a while.

She hummed a light operetta tune as she strolled along the walkway, and tugged at her new gloves, the pale peach kid with red embroidered roses climbing up the wrists. A new hat, new gloves—and a new job to do. No wonder she felt lighter! It had nothing to do with seeing Benedict again, getting to work closely with him. Nothing *at all*.

She glanced up from under her hat. The day was turning into an unusually bright one for London, the pea-souper of the last few nights lifting to reveal an actually blue sky. Well, maybe a bit more *grayish* than blue, but dotted with adorably puffy white clouds and a pale, watery peek of sunshine. Everyone else seemed to want to revel in it, too, for thicker crowds now swirled around her in both directions. A well-upholstered matron in a fur tippet and matching hat brushed past, trailed by a harried-looking maidservant loaded down with packages. A young man in a checked suit paused to give her an admiring glance, which she ignored.

She paused to study a milliner's window, all feathers and bows and straw leghorn hats laden with fruit. Next door was a bookstore/stationer, a favorite shop of hers as it always kept the newest detective novels and penny dreadfuls back for her.

She was always still astounded that *this* was where she lived. A place with clean streets and fine carriages, prosperous shops. So different from where she grew up, the fetid courts scented with cabbage and refuse, crowded rooms, beggars and pickpockets and never enough to eat.

She heard the clatter of the approaching omnibus, interrupting her bad memories, and it came to a stop at the corner. She leaped over a mud puddle to clamber aboard, digging a coin out of her silk reticule. It wasn't quite so crowded at that hour, and she quickly found a window seat where she could watch the city flash past and think about Lady Imogen's twisted tale. Passion, scandal, theft, romance! It was like a novel, but deliciously real. Well, "delicious" if they could find the letters before they were used for evil purposes, that was. Flora didn't want to see the fascinating Imogen, or even Benedict and his bride, hurt.

She disembarked at the end of the Evie's lane. It was quite different from the shop windows and green parks of her own neighborhood. It was dedicated only to business, tall, soot-streaked brick buildings, a few coffee houses and pubs. Everyone there seemed in a great hurry, bustling and rushing and heaving—except for a few lost souls slumped in the coffee houses, looking rejected. She wondered what bad news they'd written about that day.

Flora turned into the lobby of the *Evening Star*, not one of the finer newspapers but filled with cacophony. The clatter of printers, the constant clack of typewriters was almost drowned out by shouts and curses, a strange new sort of music. She dodged around rushing newsboys and ink-stained typesetters, secretaries in crisp shirtwaists, to make her way up the narrow back stairs. The hot air smelled thick with ink, paper, dust. It was all rush, noise-noise-noise. Very exciting, but Flora always wondered how Evie could stand it day in and out. But her friend seemed to thrive on it all.

She knocked quickly at a door at the far end of the narrow corridor before she pushed it open.

Evie, Flora's friend since she once wrote reviews of the Follies and Flora danced there, sat behind her battered old desk, her booted feet propped on its scarred edge, the hem of her tweed split skirt falling back from her muddy, stacked heel boots. Papers were towering around her; she'd obviously already been busy that day.

The light from the grubby windows turned Evie's

loose top-knot of auburn hair to fire, darker and deeper than Flora's strawberry curls. She was using her lorgnette to study a sheet of sketches, and didn't glance up. "Hmm, hello there, Flora luv," she murmured. "Come take a look at this. Amazing."

Flora peeked over Evie's shoulder, only to recoil. Evie always reeled her in with her work, but Flora had no desire to look at strangled, stabbed bodies so early in the day! "Ugh."

"Another murder in Whitechapel. That makes at least three now. Lead story in tonight's paper." She tossed the sketches onto her cluttered desk, sending up a puff of dust, and gestured Flora to one of the sagging chairs nearby. "What's your news today? I hope it's a good, juicy, ghostly one! It's all been so dull here since your diamonds business."

"This should make you happy, then, Evie dear!" Flora carefully drew off her gloves with a teasing smile, making her hurry-up friend wait. "Benedict visited me again!"

Evie gaped. "The duke? More diamonds, then?"

"Yes, the duke. And this time he brought his aunt. Lady Hastings."

Evie's eyes widened. "Really? She used to be the star of Society! She must have a score of tales to tell."

"Yes, that's the one. She's had some most intimate letters stolen, and is desperate to have them back. She begs our help, and says I have to go with her to a house party at Windermere Abbey to meet the suspects. Benedict told her what a fine job we did with the diamonds case..."

Evie gave a harsh bark of laughter. "Fine indeed! Not that it ended the way we hoped. But I have to say I'm happy as a clam to see you again, Flora, we need some new stories around here. So dull."

"Dull?" She laughed as she tapped at those gory images. She'd imagined her own life had become stale, of

21

course, but she didn't see how Evie ever could. She'd dreamed of being off the Society pages and writing real news for ages.

"Oh, you know what I mean! I need a new challenge. Maybe this is it. Aren't Windermere and his son-in-law big in politics these days?"

"I wouldn't know about that. I think so." Flora didn't say that the son-in-law and his real parentage were the big story.

Evie hurried to the row of filing cabinets along the back wall of her office, and started digging through the dusty folders. "Imogen Hastings, I knew that name was familiar. Look at these files! Her escapades were a bit before my time, but I know she was friends with absolutely everyone back then. And wasn't her sister the Duchess of Everton? They must have been chalk and cheese."

"I'll say! She's nothing like Benedict's grandmother," Flora snorted.

"Here we go." Evie pulled out two large, yellowing folders. "Behold Lady Imogen!" She held up an old photograph.

Flora remembered the old news photos Evie once found of the duchess. Benedict's grandmother, tall, full-bosomed, stately, clad in piles of diamonds and pearls over her crinoline gown. Her dark hair swept high and crowned with a diamond tiara as large and sparkling as a starry sky. Around her neck, a matching necklace, with a waterfall brooch on her satin bodice, bracelets on each gloved wrist. Sparkling as a Christmas tree at Windsor Castle with those famous Everton diamonds.

That dowager duchess—who now lived in the South of France without her diamonds—was completely different from the image of Imogen Flora studied now. Also tall, but slim as a willow, fair hair bound with ribbons, a pale dress trailing around her, lilies in her hand, a pearl necklace her only jewels. Artistic, almost scandalously simple, beautiful. Flora could definitely see why Margrave wrote her indiscreet letters.

"Ooh la la," Evie said as she studied the image. "What's she looking for now?"

"Those stolen letters," Flora said. "She thought maybe a séance could help, if not that party."

Evie turned the photo one way and the other, with a thoughtful expression on her ink-smudged face. "Give me the names of the party-goers, I'll see what I can find about them, too. I'll have to dig a bit. Do you think a séance might really help?"

Flora shrugged. "Chou Chou has been shockingly lazy lately, nothing has shown up at all. But you must come, we'll exchange information, see what we can find."

"Sounds like fun." Evie sighed. "I could definitely use some *fun* right now."

"Things aren't going so well here at work? Or maybe with Daisy?" Flora asked, mentioning the chorus girl at the Lyceum Evie had recently been fond of. She could assuredly sympathize with an impossible *tendresse*.

"I had hoped they might be, but things are, as always, a bit complicated." She tossed the folders onto her desk. "But I'll see you at the séance for sure. In the meantime, take these with you, see what you can read there. Lots of hotsy-totsy stuff about Lady Imogen, I'm sure."

"Thanks, Evie. I'll get them back to you as soon as I can." Flora tucked them away, and gave her friend a smile. "Things will be just fine with Daisy, I'm sure of it. I can feel it."

Evie laughed. "Your spirits say so?"

"Of course. They wouldn't steer us wrong, would they? In the meantime, I'm off to find an old friend of ours who might have more information."

Once Flora left the newspaper offices, she made her way briskly from the more respectable streets of shops, little parks, the scent of flowers and fresh breezes through squares. She suddenly pivoted on one corner and made a sharp turn onto another space altogether, a crooked, narrow warren of alleys and courtyards, the soot-streaked buildings built so tall, so close they blocked out all but a glimpse of the sunlight. Just like the places where she'd grown up and escaped. She pressed a lavender-scented handkerchief to her nose, and was glad she'd covered her frock with a borrowed coat of Evie's, plain gray wool to her ankles. She didn't want to call attention to herself.

She'd spent too many years in just such places, as an abandoned child, a factory worker, and finally backstage at the Follies, moving up from sweeping up sequins to dancing on the back row to the front row. Always making her way up, until she became Madame Flowerdew. But she never really forgot where she came from. Dirty, cramped streets smelling of moldy laundry, cabbage and onions. Always danger around every corner, just like those sketches at Evie's newspaper. She and Mary and Evie relied on each other in those days, and now.

She'd never dared dream of where she'd ended up, with a pretty flat and nice clothes. But she still had friends, useful friends, in alleyways. If only Hidey-Place Harry, notoriously unreliable but always supremely well-informed, would show up!

A cat dashed across the cobbles in front of her, startling her, and she gasped. Once the cat skittered away, she heard something else, a metallic "snick," the scuff of a boot. She whipped out her little pistol, a pretty thing with a mother-of-pearl handle, and spun around to face the shadows at the side of the alley. "Who is it?"

"Who d'ye think, Florrie?" a man cackled through his three cracked teeth as he stepped into the faint light. Short, wiry, gray-haired but with a strangely smooth face under his battered bowler hat. "Heard you was looking for me. Have some business for me, then?"

Flora drew in a deep breath, still nervous. "Indeed I do, Harry. How have you been keeping lately?"

He shrugged in his patched tweed jacket. "Well enough, well enough, can't complain. Rent's due soon, though."

"I can probably help you with that. I'm looking for some stolen papers. Intimate, important letters. The owner would greatly like them back, as soon as possible."

Harry looked intrigued. "Well, you've come to the right place! What sort of people would these be?"

Flora knew that she could trust Harry, despite appearances. Discretion was as part of his service as object retrieval, and his well-paying customers would no longer seek him out if he was known to be a blabber-mouth. She told him what she could of the suspects in the letter thefts.

He nodded sagely, stroking his sparse gray beard. "I might have a lead on summet like that, now you mention it."

"Already?"

"Gotta move fast when you have a hot potato, eh? You know that, Florrie."

She did indeed. "What's the word?"

"I heard from Patrick the Pirate—you know of him?"

Flora nodded. Pat once courted Mary, much to Mary's scorn. He was not as discreet in his work as Harry, but could be useful at times. "Sure."

"Someone came to him to see if he knew where to find just such papers, not a day or two after you say they were stolen from this old bird's safe. Didn't get the sense they were trying to sell them or nuthin', more like trying to find out who's seeking them out."

"And no one knows that yet?"

"Whoever it is, they're a coy one. Pat says it was a lady who wanted to find them, in black and veils, but with a young sort of voice. Small-like, thin. Like you."

Flora thought of the ladies in Imogen's tale. Belle, Jane, Marianne. Anyone else, anyone in the shadows? She sighed in frustration. How much easier it would be if she could just find those letters now, and toss them in the fire! But life for Florrie Gubbins was never quite so simple.

"Well, if you hear even a whisper of where they could be, let me know at once, Harry. Before Pat gets to his veiled lady." She handed him her card, as well as a generous stack of coins.

"Cor, fancy now, aren't we?" he cooed as he read the address on the card.

"I do try."

"So these papers must be fancy, too."

"They are of vital importance to the owner. Government secrets, it seems, as well as love-talk." Not to mention they could spoil Benedict's marriage prospects—again. "Returning them would be worth a lot, Harry. A *lot*."

He smiled, revealing those jagged teeth. "Maybe even worth a look-in at one of your seances?"

Flora was surprised. "You want a séance?"

He shrugged, trying to look innocent. It wasn't working very well. "Sure. I've always been interested in ghoulies and ghosties. Who ain't? Could be useful, especially on the streets nowdays. Need all the help we can get."

Flora thought of whoever was prowling the alleys, stabbing lone women. "I suppose so. If you bathe first."

Harry put his mittened hand on his chest, most affronted. "I know how to behave proper when I need to!"

"Hmph. Well, Lady Imogen has suggested a séance to try and contact the letter writer. I'll send you word, and you can attend."

"You're the best, Florrie, and I means that!" Harry paused. "But, er, you don't still have that little yapper, do you?"

Flora remembered the one time she'd brought Chou Chou to meet with Harry, and the pup bit his ankle when he insulted her blue-striped bows. "Chou Chou? Indeed I do, and her teeth are sharper than ever, so you'll have to watch yourself double-well."

"I can do that," he said with proper respect in his tone. He gave her an elaborate bow, and vanished into the alleyways as if he'd never been there at all.

Four

"Will you all join hands, please?" Flora, in her Madame Flowerdew guise, said in her best serious, soft, deep, mysterious "spirit connection" voice, even though she knew everyone in her audience. She was a professional, after all. She gave them all a serene, encouraging smile. This was her fifth séance of the week, but this was certainly different.

She glanced at Chou Chou, who lounged contentedly on her new velvet cushion in the corner, her paws crossed in front of her on top of her stuffed bear toy. She was calm; *too* calm. Flora was counting on the pup's gifts, tonight more than ever. She had to find a ghost who might have talked to Margrave, or even better Margrave himself.

She turned to the people around her oval, purple-draped table, their faces glowing silvery in the candlelight. Evie, Benedict, Lady Imogen, and Hidey-Place Harry in what looked like a new suit, with his face washed as promised. Mary waited in the corner with some of the séance paraphernalia, watching and ready to leap in if needed.

Even if Margrave did decide to visit, Flora wasn't sure how he would know where the letters went. Unless he snuck them away himself with his insubstantial, spec-

28

tral hands. Imogen looked so hopeful, though, so it had to be worth a try.

Benedict took his aunt's hand with a gentle smile, and she nodded bravely back. Everyone looked most expectant.

Flora gestured to Mary to lower the lamps in the corners of the room, and everything faded to that one small, flickering point of candlelight. Flora placed her fingertips on the crystal ball in front of her and closed her eyes. The chamber was always kept very warm with the fireplace and braziers, the windows muffled in dark red velvet draperies, antique tapestries of mysterious Grecian rituals on the walls, a thick red carpet underfoot. The only furniture was the mahogany table and matching straight-backed chairs, with the one console where Mary kept the equipment needed for every séance.

Flora always rather enjoyed the moment when the lights went down and the hush of expectation came over all. The sound of soft breathing around her, the warmth and hush. She concentrated her thoughts on the letters, on Chou Chou.

"We call upon the spirit world," she said. "We have great need of you!"

For a long, taut moment, all was still, like the seconds that stood still before a storm. Imogen gave a deep half-sob, and all was quiet again. Flora almost opened her eyes, but she was suddenly pinned to her chair by a cold, slippery, unseen force. The breath was knocked out of her, and the tapestries whirled against the walls. Evie gasped.

That sort of thing had only happened once before. A cold wind racing around the room, catching at window curtains and tablecloths, tearing at Flora's veil. Chou Chou barked and growled, and even unflappable Harry yelped. Flora gestured to everyone to stay where they were.

"What are you doing here again?" she cried, as the scent of country rain and brandy swirled around them.

She had been so sure they'd heard the last of *him*, that cranky old duke. She glanced at Benedict, who looked back at her in confusion.

"Nice to see you again, too, girl," a booming, disembodied voice echoed. "And you, Benedict. Not married yet, eh? How is the home farm faring?"

"Not yet, obviously, Grandfather," Benedict answered. "And the harvest looks to be a fair one this year. It should be profitable—as it would have been, with the proper attention before."

"What is it you want, Your Grace?" Flora asked. She hoped it wasn't diamonds again.

"You're looking for Lord Margrave, I think, Imogen?" the voice said, strangely quieter, almost tender. Flora wondered if even the duke had been one of Imogen's admirers.

Imogen gave an irritated frown. She didn't seem too happy to be talking to her brother-in-law again. "Yes, but you are not him, obviously. You should go talk to your wife instead of interfering here."

"I suppose it could have been any of your inamoratas who appeared," the duke huffed. "But most of them are, shall we say elsewhere, I fear. And Margrave is busy. I left my bridge game to bring a message, you can thank me later."

"Always the bridge games," Imogen snorted.

"Every Wednesday with the Prince Consort and Charlemagne. One of the old King Louis's joins us sometimes, but the man is a terrible cheat. Would never have been allowed to stay at Brook's, I tell you. But I need to get back, so there isn't much time. To find the letters, look to the father's face!" the wind howled higher again, and Chou Chou barked furiously. "And find yourself a rich wife soon, Benedict! The house will fall down around your ears if you don't, and you will fail in your duty. No time to waste!"

The wind faded. "Wait!" Imogen cried. "What about the letters? A face? What does Margrave say?"

"I told you! Look to the father's face," the duke called, his voice faint. The wind died completely, and Chou Chou sat back on her haunches, her ruff on edge.

"What does that mean?" Imogen moaned. "What father?"

Flora rose to her shaking feet, and gestured to Mary to turn up the lamps. The draperies hung crooked at the windows, and the tapestries were awry. Evie was reaching into her valise for a notebook to write everything down, and Harry looked fascinated. Flora wondered if he was going to set up his own séance business soon. Benedict comforted Imogen, who looked angry and irritated that she had been given such a non-clue clue.

"Just like my brother-in-law, he was insufferable in life and now in death," she muttered. "I must have those letters. I simply must!"

Five

"The air outside London just seems so *unhealthy*," Mary said with a loud sniff as Lady Imogen's carriage bounced along a shaded lane. "It just doesn't smell like anything. Very unnatural."

Flora laughed, and took a deep breath at the half-open window. Mary wasn't quite right—the breeze held a tinge of flowers and something green-ish from the hedgerows. But it wasn't London, with soot and the tang of the river.

She glanced across the carriage at Benedict, who sat beside his aunt. They exchanged a smile, and she wondered if he also thought of that voyage to Cornwall. Of being together amid nature's fury.

"Shall I close the window, Mary?" he asked, half-rising from the velvet cushions as the carriage swayed around a corner.

Mary gave him an admiring look. Even she, who seldom liked any men, had always thought well of Benedict. Flora couldn't blame her one bit. He did look awfully Viking-ish in the afternoon sunlight, his golden hair a bit tousled over his brow, and not at all as if they had been traveling for hours. Flora herself felt rumpled and dusty, and could use a nice, large whiskey. She smoothed the dark blue skirt of her "lady's companion" suit, disturbing a most disgruntled Chou Chou in the process.

"Oh, no, Your Grace, I'm sure it isn't far now. And it's such a warm day," Mary said.

Lady Imogen stirred from where she had been sitting very still, absorbed in thought, and looked out the window. To Flora it all looked rather same-ish, trees and more trees, gray stone walls with fields stretching beyond, thick hedgerows, houses sometimes glimpsed in the distance. She could see where Mary would doubt they could be happy living in such a place. But Imogen seemed to glimpse some landmark.

"Yes, not far now." Imogen sighed wistfully, stirring the short, dotted net veil of her fashionable hat. "There is the bell tower of the old Norman church, you see? And see on the top of that hill a little building with marble columns? Arabella's Teahouse, they called it, such a fine place to sit on a summer's day! I remember so many times..." She shook her head sadly. "It's been simply ages since I visited Windermere. But when I was young, a house party there was a glorious thing. Everyone longed for invitations. So much fun and freedom! And I was rather pretty back then, if I do say so myself. Much sought after for dancing."

"Nothing has changed in that regard, obviously, Aunt Imogen," Benedict said.

Imogen waved this away with a gloved hand, but her cheeks glowed a pleased pink. "Oh, I am a wreck now, a ruin!" That was clearly not true, even as she seemed to delight in her protests. "But I had many suitors then. Lord Killingsworth—now, he really should have been my choice, but my parents were not so keen on his smaller fortune. I wonder where he is now? And Margrave himself, my darling one. And Anthony Paddington, a thorn in my side for all these years. Even Thomas, owner of Windermere, always buried in his books and

33

his studies of King Arthur. You wouldn't think it to look at him now, but he was once quite an ardent *parfit* knight. And his daughter Marianne, lovely girl, would make such a fine match for you, Benedict, if this wretched scandal doesn't swamp us now."

"Aunt Imogen, about that marriage thing..." Benedict began with a warning note in his voice. "Marianne and I really hardly know each other."

"And now is your chance to get to know her! Faint heart and all that, Benedict." Imogen studied the lane outside with a frown. "I fear too many of them would be happy to see Margrave and me taken down a few pegs. Wretches. Well, I suppose I wasn't much of a mother to Peter, it's true. Not a mother at all. But I'll be hanged if I let anyone hurt him now." She suddenly slammed her gloved fist on the carriage seat, making Chou Chou whine. "Sorry, my dear. But I must do what I can for him now, see his life put right. It was my fault I did not destroy those letters when I could. So foolish. So unlike me."

Flora did ache for her; Imogen looked so brave but so very vulnerable in that moment.

"We will find them, I'm quite sure," Flora said. She took her little notebook from her valise. "Where should we start searching? Windermere Abbey sounds quite vast."

Imogen sighed. "Enormous, I fear. Three wings, plus the old portion of the abbey itself. And the gardens! Lord Windermere's office might be a place to begin, I hear he has several safes himself, as well as the cottage with the agent's office. Perhaps the teahouse?"

Flora thought of wide array of lock-picking instruments packed in her trunk, and nodded. One always had to be prepared in the psychic profession.

"There are so many extensive structures all over the estate," Imogen said. "An old basement once used by monks hiding from Cromwell, but now they store wine there, I believe. One of the monk's ghosts might be of help! If Anthony Paddington is to visit, Lord Windermere will have to be well-stocked to not be dried out of house and home, so he might make use of that space for hiding things."

Benedict laughed. "Likes to tipple, does Sir Anthony?"

Imogene snorted. "Has been ever since we were in our first Seasons! It was one reason I refused to marry him. Who wants their marital chamber to smell like a brewery every night?"

Flora and Mary giggled, and even Chou Chou seemed to smile in wry agreement.

"We will have to search those towers and cottages, as well as any library or sitting rooms, I suppose," Imogen said.

"And the out-buildings," Mary added. "I knew a smuggler who hid his hoard in the cow-shed once! No one wants to dig through muck, do they?"

She and Flora both shivered, imagining searching through such noisome products. Hopefully, it was just locked away in a nice, tidy safe.

Imogen tapped her fingertip thoughtfully on her chin. "I do wonder that Margrave sent the duke of all people to make contact at the séance. They quite despised each other in life. Is the duke your particular spirit medium, Flora?"

Flora shuddered to imagine dealing with Benedict's grandfather on a regular basis. "I don't really have a particular contact, Lady Imogen, and it definitely wouldn't be the duke. I've only had the, er, pleasure of meeting him a few times, and I'd hoped he was gone for good after the Petrie business."

Benedict groaned, and closed his eyes. "As did we all. Maybe he has found the milk of human kindness now, and just wants to help us out a bit?"

Flora wished she could believe that, but it seemed

spirits were much the same after death as they were before. "We can try another séance as soon as we're settled at Windermere," she said, though she sure actually meeting the possible culprits and trying to winnow out their secrets would be better. Of course, such people were often close-mouthed to their "inferiors," but also they didn't usually even notice them, so a companion's guise would do her well.

Being invisible did have its uses. She wished it was a psychic gift she could summon up.

"But whatever did he mean about looking to the father's face?" Imogen said, twisting a handkerchief between her fingers in worry. "Which father? Margrave? How can we, the man is dead!"

"Who are the fathers that will be at the Abbey?" Flora asked.

Imogen's eyes narrowed thoughtfully. "Peter, of course. He and Belle, though they've never really gotten along, have managed to have two little ones. My grandchildren, I suppose." She seemed quite surprised by the novel idea of grandchildren. "Thomas has Belle and Marianne. Windermere isn't entailed, so Marianne will have a large inheritance." She shot Benedict a raised-eyebrow glance, but he stared out the carriage window. "Anthony had a daughter, but she went off to India years ago. Roger, Margrave's nephew, has twin sons, they quite take after his wife Adele, horrid little spoiled creatures. So—any of them, really. But why look to their faces?"

The carriage swing around a corner and launched through an open pair of most impressive gates. Tipped with gold and enameled with an elaborate "W" surrounded by unicorns and fleurs-de-lys, they shone blindingly in the sunlight. The glare was immediately drowned in gray shades as the road led between rows of towering old oaks. The gardens were cunningly planted to reveal glimpses of the house and outbuildings, little enticing glances, dappled in light and shade. In the distance, Flora saw the teahouse atop a hill, and just across from that a red brick tower with large windows. All most impressive.

Even Mary grew silent as they rolled slowly through the theatrical grounds, the groves of trees and flashes of color from flower-strewn meadows. It felt almost like something out of Shakespeare, *As You Like It* or maybe *A Midsummer Night's Dream*, something sylvan and mysterious. Flora expected Puck to drop out of a treetop at any moment and land atop their carriage! It was all magical and beautiful, unlike anything she'd ever really known in her life, and she found herself drifting down into some kind of enchantment.

She glanced over at Benedict, who also watched the scene with an unreadable, almost dreamlike expression. She wondered if he saw how it could one day be his, if he married this Marianne. That this could be his life as it could never be Flora's. She hugged Chou Chou closer, and remembered Harry's warning that these letters would not just affect Imogen and her secret son, but were of international importance if the scandals written there were revealed. That and the grand estate were almost overwhelming.

They suddenly tumbled out of shade into sunlight again, buttery and glowing as if to bestow benediction on the house below. It was indeed vast, just as Imogen said. The center section was the old abbey, with stone walkways and pointed arches, stained glass windows monks could almost be peering out of to see who invaded their sanctuary. Cloister walks stretched to either side, giving little glimpses of gardens beyond. Chou Chou growled low in her throat as if she sensed spirits drifting there, their ghostly sandals silent on old flagstone floors. Covered walkways connected to the newer wings, perfect Palladian style with symmetrical windows and pale marble faced in darker brick.

The carriage drove around a large Italian fountain in the center of the graveled drive, topped with a statue of Diana the huntress holding her gilded bow aloft while streams splashed around her in welcoming music. They drove past the old abbey and its ghosts to the entrance of one of the newer wings, two staircases sweeping up to a row of columns and a shaded portico leading to the front doors where rows of servants waited. Formal gardens spread beyond, roses and ivy and rolling, bright green lawns.

The Windermeres certainly didn't look as if they needed to resort to blackmail, if that was what someone intended with the letters. The Abbey was gorgeous, beautifully maintained by those rows of servants waiting at the doors. What could be their motive in wanting the letters? A political grudge? Old romantic stings? Flora thought if she had such a house, she would lock herself inside and never deal with people and their messes again!

"They haven't done so badly for themselves over the years, have they?" Imogen mused. A footman in blue and gold livery hurried out to unlock the carriage doors and lower the steps before reaching for Imogen's hand. Flora noticed he was a handsome young man, with most enticing dimples set below carved cheekbones, and Imogen flashed him a flirty smile. "Not so badly at all."

Once she stood on the gravel of the drive, Benedict helped Mary and Flora to alight. Flora smiled up at him as she held Chou Chou against her. "Just think, dukie. This could all be yours."

"Ha," he answered.

"Lady Hastings," a portly man in a butler's well-cut dark coat said in a booming voice, bowing low. "I am Henton, butler here at Windermere Abbey, and this is the housekeeper, Mrs. Appleton. We are most happy to welcome you back to the house after such a long time between visits."

"Anything you require while you are here, Lady

Hastings, anything at all, please do call for me at once," Mrs. Appleton, whose pink cheeks echoed her name, said with a curtsy.

"Thank you. I know I shall soon require a bath." Imogen marched up the steps, with Flora, Mary, and Benedict hurrying to follow as Henton and Mrs. Appleton scrambled to properly greet the duke. "Are we the first to arrive?"

"Lord Margrave has arrived—the *new* Lord Margrave," Henton said. "Lady Margrave arrived separately."

Flora remembered they were estranged, and Peter's beautiful mistress was a spanner in the works of this all. She wondered how it would all go when they had to meet up. Like a drawing room operetta, it all was.

"And Mrs. Annis?"

Henton's lips pursed. "Mrs. Annis has not yet arrived. Nor have Mr. and Mrs. Margrave." So the nephew and his ambitious wife weren't there yet.

"Ah, a reprieve," Imogen sound wryly.

They stepped into the cool shade of the house, a grand entrance built to impress, as it mightily did. Flora tried not to gape at it all, at the split, cantilevered staircase unlike anything she'd seen before. It swept up either side of the pink and white marble hall, its ironwork balustrade elaborately wrought with flowers and vines, leading up to a round, columned walkway that echoed the outside entrance. A skylight dome was high overhead, bathing the whole scene in mellow light that shone on statues in their niches, and on elaborate plasterwork fashioned into more flowers, wreaths and bouquets.

At the top of the stairs, Henton inclined his head toward one of the doorways that opened off the landing. "Lord Windermere and Lady Marianne are serving tea in the Cream Sitting Room, my lady. I shall see that your luggage has been taken to your suite, and a bath drawn in the meantime. If your maid would care to come with me?" He nodded to Mary.

"What a treasure you are, Henton," Imogen said, making the man beam. She held out her hand for Benedict's arm, and led the way into the sitting room.

Flora hoisted Chou Chou higher into her arms and started to follow, when she glimpsed a strange structure beyond one of the windows. It was low and elegant, church-like with a bell tower and pointed window embrasures, but not like an old abbey. It was surrounded by large stones and even a pyramid.

"What an interesting place," she murmured.

"The family chapel," Mrs. Appleton offered. "For private worship, and family internment. The pyramid was the last Lord Windermere."

"Most striking." Flora noticed the teahouse atop a hill, and the red brick tower opposite. "And that strange tower, Mrs. Appleton?"

Mrs. Appleton's eyes narrowed, as if something about the tower wasn't quite proper. Maybe it just needed more cleaning than she would like. "Lady Marianne's scientific observatory. She has many studies, you see. She is there most days—and evenings. Such havoc with mealtimes."

"Science?" Flora said, intrigued by this glimpse of Benedict's possible future bride. She sounded rather more interesting than some deb who just served tea and went dancing. "Is she perhaps a botanist of some sort? The gardens here are so lovely."

Mrs. Appleton gave a little snort. "I have no idea what her ladyship does in there. She never lets anyone inside, even to dust. Most inconvenient."

Flora nodded, and noticed the glint of something bright on one of the high tower windows, maybe a telescope of some sort. She was fascinated, but there was no time to ponder it, as Imogen called her into the sitting room.

~

To call such a space a mere "sitting room" seemed funny indeed, Flora thought as she studied the chamber she stepped into. It was more like a warehouse of grandeur, a long, narrow, high room lined with tall windows on one side, looped and draped in gold satin, and bookshelves on the other. A painted ceiling, gods and goddesses and cupids peeking down from white clouds limned with gold leaf, loomed overhead, while the blue and green antique carpet was dotted with brocade chairs. At the very far end, a carved fireplace lurked, with a gathering of people around it. It was beautiful room, mind-boggling even, but so cold it made Chou Chou shiver in Flora's arms.

It felt like a walk that took miles as Flora followed Imogen and Benedict along the length of the floor. She wasn't a girl to be easily intimidated; she'd spent years facing down theater managers and diva leading ladies, not to mention recently cranky ghosts and haughty duchesses. Yet she something so chilly, so fluttery, her feet heavy on the plush carpet.

She thought of debs she'd read about in the Society pages of Evie's papers, even met a few when they timidly crept in for a séance, and what they went through in Court presentations. She and Mary always laughed at them a bit. All those towering feathers, long trains, low, creaky-kneed curtsies, and tiptoeing backwards from the no-doubt bored silly queen! It sounded like something from a cheap musicale where the ingenue would fall top-over-tail into a prince. But the girls found it deadly serious, terrified that a misstep would ruin their lives forever.

Now she understood how they felt. The eyes of everyone in that still, silent tableau at the end of the never-ending room seemed fixed in her direction, as if looking for fault. Even Chou Chou had gone very quiet.

Flora told herself sternly they couldn't possibly be looking at *her*, she was just the lady's companion, part of the carpet and the silk wallpaper but nearly as important. They surely watched Benedict and Lady Imogen.

One man broke away from the grouping and strode forward. He was tall, lean, surely very handsome in his youth, and still clearly proud of his silvery hair, which he wore unfashionably long. He wore a yellow brocade cap atop that mane, and a matching robe, as if he tried to match the medieval grandeur of the house. "Lady Hastings. Imogen. It has been too, too long since you graced our presence."

Flora guessed he must be Lord Windermere, owner of that vast palace. He did look like his home, with all that brocade and hair! She'd have cast him as the ghost of the first owner if she were writing a play about the place, a man eternally tormented by the spirits of the monks he had dispossessed.

"Thomas. Yes, indeed. I remember when you were in short pants, and we dashed around here as children! And then *later*," Imogen answered, coolly turning up her cheek for his greeting kiss. "Your father was quite furious when you played pranks as a boy. He even turned you over his knee right in front of the whole tea party, in this very room! My parents often laughed about it."

Thomas flushed an angry red at such a reminder of a childish peccadillo. Or maybe, Flora mused, he did not want a lady he once courted remembering *that* about him. "Those days are quite, quite behind me, I do assure you. I hope we have other memories of the Abbey now." He waved a young lady forward. "I fear my daughter Belle, your godson's wife, though he may not remember it, is not here yet. But you know my youngest, Marianne. I am sure of that." He winked—winked!--at Benedict as he took his daughter's hand. "And I *know* the duke has made her acquaintance."

Marianne Windermere, on the other hand, was not someone Flora would have cast as "duchess" in her play. And not just because Benedict would be the bridegroom in question. She was very tall, and could be elegant, but she tended to stoop in an unflattering pale green muslin gown, and her dark hair was piled untidily atop her head and fastened with—was that a *pencil*? She had very blue eyes behind glinting spectacles, and they looked down shyly. "Lady Hastings. Your Grace."

Benedict gave her a kind smile. "Lady Marianne. So good to see you again. I believe we last met at the Woodwards' Venetian breakfast party."

"Yes. Indeed," she said briefly, so softly she could barely be heard, not looking at Benedict. Her father glared, and gave her a sharp nudge. Flora thought it looked like this match might be going the way of the Petrie one. But then, how could a young lady who lived in such a house with such a father, swaddled in marble and gilt and satin and liveried servants, but with no free will, have much spirit in them? Flora felt terribly sorry for her, despite all Marianne had.

Marianne glimpsed Chou Chou, and a great change fell over her like a sunbeam on a gray day. Her eyes widened, and her cheeks flared pink with delight. "Oh! What a darling puppy! Isn't it the dearest thing ever? May I pet it?" She took a step toward Flora, then seemed to doubt herself, going still.

"Of course! This is Chou Chou, your ladyship," Flora said. She certainly couldn't help but warm to anyone who appreciated Chou Chou's great charm. Chou Chou played her part, preening a bit, peeking up at Marianne from large, amber eyes. "Would you care to pet her, then?"

"May I really?" Marianne reached out an eager hand.

"Marianne," her father snapped. "You know my view of animals in the house."

Marianne surprisingly ignored him, to Flora's surprise. She wasn't often wrong about people. In all the lines of work she'd ever had, a girl couldn't afford to misjudge others too often. But Marianne did surprise her. She reached out and firmly patted Chou Chou's fluffy little head, cooing. "Papa thinks all dogs belong in the kennels," she whispered. "I've always so longed for a pup of my own, a little dog to stay by my side."

"The dog is mine," Imogen said imperiously to Lord Windermere. "In the care of my companion, Miss Flora Trentham. I am sure her presence cannot be a problem, Thomas." It was emphatically a statement, not a question. Not for the first time, Flora wished she could grow up into being Lady Imogen.

Lord Windermere looked irritated, but he nodded. "Of course it is not, my dearest Imogen."

"You can visit her whenever you like, Lady Marianne," Flora whispered, and Marianne beamed.

"Do come meet the others," Lord Windermere said, offering his arm to Imogen as he led the way toward the fireplace grouping. Marianne followed him reluctantly, glancing back at Chou Chou. "You know Roger Margrave, I think."

The nephew who could be the earl, if not for Peter. "Certainly," Imogen said. Her gaze swept over the young man who leaped up from his settee, and her lips pursed. Flora guessed she found him not much like his uncle, her once-loved darling Lord Margrave, who was *virile* and *vital*. Like Marianne, he seemed stooped and shy, cast in some shade that prevented him from flowering. But he had kind eyes beneath a ruffled fringe of pale hair. Flora wondered if he could really have broken into a safe and snatched some indiscreet letters. He didn't seem the sort, in the play she now wrote in her mind.

But then, what could a man do if he thought an earldom was at stake?

"Lady Imogen," he said with a tentative smile. "You haven't formally met my wife, Adele, I think."

A lady seated next to him on the settee nodded at them, but did not rise. Now, *she* Flora could imagine providing every ambition her husband lacked, even up to prying open a safe. She looked like a galleon in sail, bosomy and creamy in a fashionable tea dress of lilac silk and chiffon, her cat-like green eyes taking in everything. The lady crackled with energy, but not positive, vital, life-giving energy. On-edge, needy lightning cracks of energy.

"Lady Hastings," she drawled. How very—interesting to meet you. I have long heard so much of you. Such a—a *fascinating* life you have led."

"It's not quite over yet, my dear," Imogen said dryly.

"And this must be your dear nephew, the *duke*," Adele said, in a very different, almost fawning tone. "We have certainly much of *you*, sirrah."

Benedict looked abashed. "I—I am very pleased to meet you, Mrs. Margrave."

Thomas "harrumphed," and Adele pulled Roger down beside her again. "And this is Jane Annis, a newcomer to our neighborhood, but most welcome as tenant of Rose Lodge. A widow, and so kind of her to grace our little gathering." He shot a lady who sat half in shadow a lustful stare, leaning toward her as if she could not help himself.

Flora could see why he might, even though Jane Annis was said to be his own daughter's rival in romance. Mrs. Annis was a great beauty indeed, with raven-black hair against very fair skin, her sky-blue eyes glowing. And now she was a neighbor of Windermere Abbey, as well as Peter's lover! It seemed rather odd she might be at such a party, but Flora thought now that perhaps it was Lord Windermere's doing, if he lusted after Mrs. Annis himself. Or maybe Jane Annis was there because she knew what was afoot and wanted to help Peter—or harm him. Her enigmatic little smile gave nothing at all away, and Flora had to admire how well she played her part.

It would be fascinating to see how such a tangled web played out. She did enjoy reading about complicated passions, as long as they were on the page and not in her own life.

"Lady Imogen. How very pleased I am to meet you at long last," Jane said in a soft, purring voice. But her smile seemed sincere as she beamed up at Imogen. "And Your Grace. They never did say how handsome you are. It must run in your family, such fine looks."

Benedict blushed. *Blushed*! "You are too kind, Mrs. Annis."

Imogen smirked at them all. "My nephew is indeed admired wherever he goes. As are you, I am sure, Mrs. Annis."

Jane smiled sweetly. "People are always so kind." She slanted a glance at Adele. "*Most* people, I should say."

Adele snapped open a painted silk fan with a sharp "snick." "I merely said Lord Windermere, via Lord Margrave, keeps such an interesting guest list these days. So fascinating. Isn't that so, my dear?" She grabbed up her husband's arm with her free hand, holding him close.

"Yes, yes, my love. F—Fascinating," Roger stammered, not looking at Jane.

A few others, who it seemed had nothing to do with Imogen's stolen letters at all, were introduced, and a tea tray brought in to be arranged on the fireside table. Whatever else he was, Flora thought, Lord Windermere wasn't a skin-flint about his catering. The tiered trays of Sèvres porcelain were stacked high with sandwiches, salmon and cucumber and egg, as well as iced cakes, hot-house strawberries and cream, raspberry jam, and scones. Chou Chou covetously eyed a cinnamon cake, but Flora held her very tightly as they took a seat on the outskirts of the group, where she could observe everyone.

She and Benedict and Imogen had agreed that no one would look too closely at a companion, and indeed they did not. They went back to their conversation, Adele fanning herself and holding on to her husband, Lord Windermere sitting too close to Jane. Only Marianne paid any mind, politely making sure Flora had tea and a plate of cakes, and that Chou Chou was given a discreet salmon sandwich.

The door opened once more, and Peter appeared at last. Flora fancied she could see a trace of Imogen in his handsome face, but maybe that was just imagining. He bowed and smiled, greeted everyone, and sat down beside Imogen to take a cup of tea.

"And how are your plans going for political office, Peter dear, now that you are Lord Margrave?" Imogen asked him. She watched him eagerly, but he looked at Jane, who gently touched his arm.

"It is good of you to inquire, godmother. The prime minister has spoken to me at the club several times, as has his private secretary, and even the Duke of Edinburgh, who passes on his mother's compliments to me at every chance, which is very flattering," Peter said carefully. "They have all discreetly expressed their support if I should wish to launch a campaign of sorts…"

"Wish?" Imogen said sharply. "Your father would have been out day and night gathering allies, my dear boy! It was his greatest wish to see you make a great name for yourself."

And Lady Imogen's greatest wish, too, Flora was sure, as she examined the pair of them, secret mother and son. They had the same eyes, dark as night, but Peter's were gentle, inward-peering, while Imogen's always sparkled and danced with mischief and interest. She wondered how much Peter would truly care if he was no longer the earl. Maybe he wanted to join Jane at Rose

Lodge, not seek allies at his club. Maybe he had even taken the letters himself!

"I've been busy looking after the estate, godmother," he said quietly, and placed his hand over Jane's with a smile. "Margrave Hall requires much attention just now. Your kind party in honor of my father was the first time I had visited London in some weeks."

"The country air has been so good for Peter, truly, Lady Hastings," Jane said. "And the people on the estate do love him so!"

"With your help, I am sure, Mrs. Annis," Adele snapped. She stuffed a strawberry in her mouth.

"Rose Lodge is not so far from Margrave Hall, that is true," Jane answered softly. "I enjoy seeing what happens in my neighborhood. The life here suits us—that is, suits Peter."

Interesting, Flora thought. She would have imagined Jane would want her lover to rise high, before any scandal broke. But maybe not everyone could be predicted in that way. Not everyone wanted power and fame. Maybe Jane wanted something else entirely. Or maybe she was a fine actress. The Lyceum's loss.

"Well," Imogen said. "There is plenty of time, I am sure. Your father has not been gone long and must be mourned. And you do have so many friends who stand ready to help you at any moment."

"As long as he behaves himself as he ought," Lord Windermere snapped.

Imogen ignored him. "Just do not leave it too long, my dear boy. Time waits for no man, and the country needs you." She turned to speak to Marianne, who had been silently slipping Chou Chou bits of scone.

Tea was nearly finished, everyone gathering themselves to retire before dinner, when the double doors of the sitting room were flung open with a loud bang. Chou Chou growled, and a silence fell over the little gathering as everyone turned to stare at such a disruption to their regular, ordered, comfortable world. A man strode forward, portly, bald, a cane swinging in his gloved hand, taking them all in with a laughing glance.

Imogen stiffened, and Benedict reached for her hand.

This whole party made Flora feel she'd been tossed back to her theater days, with passions and hatreds bubbling up and pushed down, people hating and loving each other, secrets thick in the air. Words unsaid at every turn.

The man bowed low before Imogen, and caught up her free hand to place a kiss on it. She snatched it away, and he laughed.

"I do apologize for my late arrival," the man announced to the room at large, rolling his r's like he was in a bad production of Shakespeare.

"Not at all," Lord Windermere said, clearly as disgruntled by the tardiness as he'd been by Chou Chou. "We were just finishing tea. You are most welcome, Sir Anthony."

"I should hope so, Windermere!" the man growled. "I have traveled all this way, I should hope you could extend some hospitality for once." He turned to Imogen and leaned closer to her, making her lean back with a frown. "And Imogen. As lovely as ever, I see. I hope we can spend a great deal more time together this week..."

Sir Anthony Paddington, then. One of Imogen's former lovers. Flora wondered what such a formidable lady ever saw in him, he seemed so strutting and loud. But who knew what anyone saw in anyone else? What happened in the past that carried into the future, and what was left there, hopefully to sink without a trace.

~

Flora wasn't sure what to expect of her "companion's" chamber. Maybe a garret, like in an opera, tiny and cold and cramped, high under the eaves. Or a closet tucked into some nook. Yet Imogen had insisted she must have Flora, "Miss Trentham," close to her, so she was, just beyond Imogen's grand satin bedchamber in a guest suite at the front of the house. A large bed was draped in cheerful, bright chintz hangings that matched the window curtains and the cushions on the chairs and dressing table bench, while a small, white stone fireplace overlaid with a floral-carved mantel promised coziness on chillier nights. A pink and white carpet stretched underfoot, and a dressing table was trimmed in lace and spread with an array of lotions and powders in pink glass bottles.

"Not so bad, eh, lamb-kins?" she said to Chou Chou, as she deposited the dog in the middle of the bed. Chou Chou stretched out her paws experimentally, turned around three times, and plopped down, as if satisfied.

"No ghosties, then?" Flora opened the window draperies. The gravel driveway spread below her, and Diana's fountain, just as it should be. Only the distant glimpse of the chapel and its graveyard, bathed now in rosy-gold sunset light, struck a spooky note. She watched the sun sink lower, casting the sky into violet-inky darkness and the house glow out into it all.

She thought about everyone she'd just met. She did like Imogen a great deal; the lady was strong and independent, she'd lived her life as she chose and did not apologize for it, and she cared about the people she had made her family. Yet Flora couldn't quite see how she could help Imogen with her quest. Windermere Abbey was huge; if the letters still existed, they could be anywhere, with anyone. They all seemed to have reasons to have old secrets buried or, conversely, dug up. And the late duke, just like last time, had hardly been a help from the other side of the veil. Look to the father's face, indeed!

"What do you think, Chou Chou?" she asked as she turned back to the chamber. The pup, still lounging in the center of the bed, blinked and rolled over. Her little paws kicked in the air.

"Well, don't get too accustomed to such swish surroundings, you spoiled beastie. We have work to do here!"

The little ormolu clock on the pale marble fireplace mantel chimed the hour, just as a gong resonated along the corridors, and Flora realized she'd have to get dressed for dinner in a hurry, even if Mary didn't appear soon to help. She opened the trunk that had been delivered by a footman, and sorted through the contents with not much enthusiasm. All her best gowns had been left behind, all those pretty bright silks and chiffons! Instead there were respectable "lady's companion" costumes, gray and dark green and blue. No dash at all.

She held up a dinner frock of forest green muslin trimmed with black braid, and decided it would have to do.

There was still no Mary, and no maid of the house to help her, no doubt all of them busy with important guests. But Flora hadn't been at the Follies for so long for nothing. Backstage, costume changes were lightning-quick in the middle of corridors between scenes. Princesses turning to servants and vice versa. She managed to get herself into the gown, and tidied her hair in front of the dressing table mirror. Not much to be done about its not-respectable red hue, but she pinned it back tight and covered what she could with a little black cap. She turned her head this way and that, examining the effect, and decided it would have to do.

By then, it was full dark outside. She went to peer outside, at the way the house's many windows cast an almost daylight sheen on the gardens, and noticed one of her windows opened onto a small balcony. Several of the little, Juliet-style porticos lined up along the wall.

She pushed open the tall glass casement and slipped out onto the tiny, stone space, taking in the view around her. XXX

"Pssst! Flora!" she heard someone call, and she instinctively leaped back, half-sure a ghost had followed her.

But it was no spectral monk or goblin. It was Benedict, standing below her balcony just like the Juliet scene she'd imagined, blending into the shadows in his dark evening suit. His golden hair shimmered in the light from her window, and she leaned toward him in a sudden rush of yearning.

But she couldn't afford to *yearn* for anything. "What are you doing?" she called back, glancing around to see if anyone watched. They seemed to be alone.

"A bit of reconnaissance, of course," he said. "We'll have a lot of ground to cover to find 'the father's face' of Aunt Imogen's letters, don't you think? Come down! We can take a quick turn around the garden before dinner, get the lay of the land."

He sounded excited, almost boyish, and she smiled to remember their adventures in France and Cornwall. How grand it had all been! How she would love to find that joie de vivre all over again. "How do I get down?"

"The same way I escaped my own balcony over there! See this trellis?" He shook an ivy-covered structure below her.

She looked back at Chou Chou, who was now faintly snoring in her soft bed. She lifted the hem of her dull dress, and clambered over the balustrade to find her footing on the trellis. It shook a bit under her weight, the ivy leaves trembling, but she felt some of that old Flora Flowerdew, Chorus Girl, boldness come back to her, like prancing onto stage into the hiss of the footlights amid applause and shouts. Kicking and spinning and twirling. But now she only had an audience of one. The most important one. Benedict.

He caught her before she reached the ground, spinning her a bit with her feet off the ground until she giggled like a schoolgirl. Holding hands, they dashed off into the night, laughing together as if they had gotten away with something.

"I don't think I've ever felt quite like a naughty schoolgirl escaped from lessons," she gasped. Not that she'd ever had any schoolroom lessons.

He laughed, that rich, dark sound so full of freedom she remembered too well. "Nor have I. I could seldom get out from under my tutor's eye, and once I went to school—there was never any escape. Not like this!"

"I don't know where to even begin here," Flora said, examining the rows and rows of amber-lit windows, the forest of chimneys.

"I found something, one of the maids told me about it. Very chatty she was, most attentive, I think she was neglecting one of her chores, the housekeeper was quite cross," he said, and Flora couldn't blame the maid for getting flirty and forgetting everything about her work when she looked into his eyes. "Come on! You'll love it, just like those caves we saw."

"A sea cave? Here?" They hurried along a pathway, the gravel glowing in the moonlight, between trees that bent over their heads. She thought of the Cornwall caves, the rush of the water, the green-salt smell.

"Not exactly." He led her around a corner, and they suddenly faced a small lake, the water glassy under the stars. At the far end of the water, a derelict boathouse loomed up, the roof sagging, old rowing vessels piled up around it, strangely unkempt for such a grand place where everything else seemed kept in its place. Benedict found a half-open window and shoved it upward. He caught the crumbling sill and pulled himself up and over, unconcerned by his evening attire. He was never the usual sort of duke.

"Come on, Flora, I'll boost you up," he called as he leaned back outside, holding out his hand to her.

She peered closer at the building. It seemed like it was about to topple over into the water at any moment. More like a shack than anything. "Are you sure?"

He grinned down at her. "Scared of any ghosts here?"

"Chou Chou isn't here to tell me about them, so not really. I might be scared it will fall into that lake." She glanced over her shoulder, and thought she saw a flashing, flittering movement along the shore. But it seemed only a shadow. "If ghosts drift around anywhere, surely it's here at Windermere."

"Well, maybe it's some medieval knights and ladies, staging a ye olde tyme joust! That could be fun. I played Falstaff once at school, you know. I could join in the revels."

"You! Falstaff?" she cried, and giggled all over again. She tried to picture him fat and jolly, reveling around tavern, but the vision wouldn't quite appear. She turned away and peeked in the window, standing on tiptoe. The dirt-streaked floor was mostly empty, with just a rotting old rowing boat, a pile of ropes, and, promisingly, rows of old trunks.

"I was quite good at Falstaff," he huffed. "Everyone said so. Now are you coming inside or not?"

She certainly didn't want to look like a scaredy-cat in front of him. "Oh, very well, but it has to be quick." She let him boost her up through the open window, and she leaped past the splintered old windowsill to land on a dusty floor. Benedict pulled himself up after her, falling to the floor with a thud and a roll that made him laugh. When he jumped up, he looked adorably rumpled, and she laughed.

"You'll look quite the rogue in front of Lady Marianne," she tsked, trying to smooth down a wild lock of hair. "That will never do!"

He arched his brow at her. "Will I? How does it matter?"

"Didn't your aunt say she'd make a fine duchess? She does seem rather nice. Chou Chou likes her. And she could be very pretty." Flora smiled wistfully at the thought, her hand gone still on the silk of his hair as he stared down at her in the starlight.

"She didn't seem to like me so much. I don't think she'd care much about a dusty evening suit or rumpled hair." He turned his head and, much to her shock, pressed a kiss to the inside of her wrist. The touch of it tingled and sparked, and she drew away with a gasp. In the distance, a bell rang, instructing everyone to dress for dinner, breaking the spell. "We had better go in. We'll come back tomorrow to see what those trunks are all about, yes?"

"You'll be looked for at every party event, surely. It won't be easy for you to slip away."

He laughed. "Don't worry, I seldom do what I don't wish to. I'll find a way. I always do." She was quite certain he did. But even she could see that he didn't quite believe that any more. He had to be a duke sooner or later. Yet she knew this adventure wasn't over. They were kindred spirits in curiosity.

They hurried back to the pathway and turned toward the waiting house, looming over everything in the night. Surely whatever they sought had to be behind its serene-looking walls, somewhere.

Six

The dining room was as grand as the rest of the house, maybe even more so, Flora thought as she examined it all from her seat at the far end of the cricket-pitch length table. The mahogany length, spread with fine white damask and laid with gold-edged, flower-painted china, gilt vases filled with roses, heavy silverware, shining crystal wineglasses, stretched into infinity along a dark red carpet, past red brocade-papered walls lined with portraits of scowling Windermere ancestors. Footmen were behind almost every chair, waiting to leap into action at any slight gesture.

Jane reached out to softly touch Lord Windermere's sleeve, laughing at some remark he'd made, her lovely face glowing in the candlelight. Peter stared at her, entranced. "Such a house must be terribly haunted, Thomas," she said, in her soft, caramel-smooth voice. Flora quite envied her. She would have made a smash on the stage. "One does hear such tales of the Abbey. Gray ladies in the corridors, monks in the cloister walk, a wolf howling at the full moon in the gardens..."

Lord Windermere also laughed, watching her closely over the edge of his gold-rimmed wineglass. Flora wondered if he, too, was in love with the gorgeous Mrs. Annis, despite the havoc she seemed to be wreaking in his daughter's life. "Oh, my dear lady, you must not believe all you have heard. People do love a romantic tale, the spookier the better. All old houses make their strange cracks and creaks, it's good to keep the name of the estate of interest. There is much history in these walls, I would not be surprised some past inhabitants might be reluctant to leave."

"Grandmama used to tell us tales of tunnels that run under the old abbey," Marianne said. "Perhaps the sounds come from that. I do recall Grandmama was sure there were the ghosts of smugglers in the tunnels."

Her father shot her a small frown. "My mother was a fanciful lady, always scribbling poetry and such. Smugglers, indeed! And I thought you considered yourself a scientist of some sort!"

"A scientist?" Benedict asked her, and she turned to answer him, her pale face almost glowing pink. From the handsome man—or science?

"Yes, I am interested in..." she began.

"Oh, my dear Lady Marianne, what a lot of trouble," Jane said with a merry, teasing twinkle that made Marianne scowl. "I find myself so busy with household matters, with helping neighbors in their times of trouble, I could hardly have time to study anything so complicated. As would most ladies."

"We ladies must keep ourselves busy somehow," Imogen said wryly, reaching for her wineglass. "Embroidery, maybe. Miss Trentham there is a gifted medium. I find it very useful."

"Oh, such fun," Jane cried. "We must have a séance one of our evenings here. I am sure I would adore them, one does hear such amazing things."

Peter shot her a worried glance. "You never know, Jane, what might come of such things. We should be cautious."

"Indeed," Imogen murmured. "Sometimes the past should merely stay in the past."

57

Adele protested as a footman offered her the filet en croute. "Oh, no. Sometimes the past has *vital* importance to the present. Is that not so, Roger?"

Suddenly, the dining room door opened, and Henton appeared, looking rather perturbed. He slowly approached Lord Windermere at the head of the table. "My lord," he said quietly, but Flora's ears were acute. "Another guest has just arrived."

Lord Windermere looked puzzled, and not at all happy to be taken away from watching the beauteous Mrs. Annis. "Surely we are all here?"

"She was insistent you wanted her to be present..."

A lady swept around the footmen stationed at the door, and struck a grand pose, quite as if she were making a Lady Macbeth entrance at Covent Garden. Marianne stiffened, and Windermere scowled.

Peter leaped up so quickly his chair almost toppled onto the polished parquet floor. Neither he nor Jane looked at all happy. Surely if this were indeed a theater they would complain of their seats and demand a ticket refund, but everyone else seemed fascinated.

"Belle," Peter said.

Flora also turned to stare at the lady in great interest. So this was Peter's estranged wife, Lord Windermere's other daughter, though he seemed to have forgotten she was attending the party. She was tall, like her sister Marianne, but there the resemblance ended. Belle was buxom in her red travel suit and large, feathered hat, bright blonde curls peeking out from its lacy trim, her gray eyes overly bright as she swept a long glance over the company.

"I am sure a husband has no interest in attending a party at such a *respectable* house as my father keeps without his wife," she said, and Flora could practically hear the stage thunder that should accompany her. "Papa has said I am welcome here at any time, unlike my own home, and here I am. Did you forget my arrival time, Papa?"

It was clear Lord Windermere had, for he stared and harrumphed and seemed rather lost for once.

"My lord, should we then set another place?" Henton asked. "The next course is soon to be served."

"Certainly, yes, of course. Thank you, Henton," Lord Windermere answered. "Of course I, er, remembered you were coming, Belle."

"Dear Papa," she said with a sticky-sweet smile, and sailed forward to kiss his cheek, ignoring Jane at his other side. She unpinned her hat and tossed it at Henton, who looked at it as if a snake had landed in his hands. "I knew you would not mind my late arrival. And, Marianne, how—interesting you look tonight."

Despite her doubtful glance at Marianne's pale yellow muslin dress, her careless words, Marianne beamed at her. "It's so good to see you again, Belle!"

"Then you should visit me more in London, sister. A lady so put upon in life needs her family around her." Belle smoothed the sleeve of her red traveling suit, and tossed her head. "I am hardly dressed for dinner, but what is such a matter among friends?" Henton had directed a place be set halfway down the table, but Belle just sat down next to Peter and beamed at him. "Darling, it's been so very long! You must tell me *all* you have been doing, I am sure it is utterly fascinating."

~

Escaping to the sitting room was a relief after the last, tense courses over the dinner table, Flora thought as she sipped at a cup of coffee from her chair in the corner and studied the ladies gathered around. Belle and Marianne talked by one of the windows, or rather Belle talked, waving her hands in a most animated fashion as Marianne nodded.

Imogen and Jane studied the sheet music at the piano opposite Flora's corner, neither of them giving any clue as to how they felt about the little scene in the dining room.

But Flora was not alone long. To her surprise, Adele Margrave swept across the room in a flurry of blue silk and sat down beside her. She snapped open her lace fan.

"Is it true that you can perform seances, Miss, um..." Adele asked.

"Miss Trentham," Flora answered, in what she hoped was a suitably quiet "companion" tone. "Only for a hobby. I fear I have little true gift."

"Still, it must be very useful. I should like to know what the spirits would predict about my future! Have you worked long for Lady Imogen, then, Miss, um, Trentham?" Adele asked, with a smile that rather reminded Flora of a circus tiger baring its teeth. Still, surely Adele, who was said to be ambitious for her husband and would love to be a countess, ought to have a great deal of interesting information about this odd gathering of family and friends that hardly seemed worthworthy of such a name.

"Not for very long, Mrs. Margrave," Flora answered, and took a demure sip of tea. "She is an excellent employer."

"Ah, yes, I am sure." Adele also sipped her drink, looking rather unconvincingly wide-eyed. "A veritable pillar of Society, one does hear. I believe she was great friends with my Roger's uncle."

Flora tilted her head to examine Adele, considering how to answer. It seemed the lady tried to winkle information out of her just as Flora did. She had to be careful. She'd often found in her Madame Flowerdew work that simply letting silence reign, letting it stretch out until it had to be filled, could tell her so much. Could give time to observe.

"When I married my husband, I was sure he was meant for great things," Adele said, her tone mingled anger and sadness. Frustration. Flora could sympathize. It was never easy for women of any class, waiting for their destinies to be decided by others. To be moved one way or the other by men. "Such an earl he would have made! He was the heir to his uncle when he was a child, you know, and had begun to be prepared in such fine ways. Education, connections. Poor Roger..." She tsked softly, and glanced across the room to examine Jane's lovely face. The lady was trying to be serene, to keep smiling, yet even there, written in the lines beside her lightly rouged lips, was a tense awareness of Belle. Of the taut air in the drawing room. "It would be such a scandal, of course, for the entire family, and one my husband would never have brought upon us. A *divorce*! No matter how the Prince of Wales behaves, it is no thing for respectable people. Wouldn't you agree?"

Especially when property and titles were involved, Flora was sure. "I would not wish it upon anyone," she murmured. And she would not. Divorce caused such trouble for people. But then again, wouldn't freedom at any cost be better? People like the Windermeres and Margraves had concerns and options everyone else could only dream of. Perhaps Adele hoped in some way the scandal might bring Roger to the title at last, though Flora couldn't see how that was possible. Adele would be better off trying blackmail.

"I will always help my husband. *Always*. As a dutiful wife should. Poor Belle should have realized that for herself." Adele and Flora both turned to examine Belle where she sat in the window seat with her sister. Belle was laughing, flapping her silk fan back and forth as if she had not a care in the world, but just as Jane was always aware of her, she was pointedly ignoring her rival too assiduously. "I am sure you will one day make an exemplary wife, Miss Trentham, to some respectable curate or clerk. If I may offer some advice?"

"Please do," Flora said mildly.

"Choose most carefully. I fear Lady Imogen could not be of any help in such a vital endeavor. The life she has led!" Adele's eyes narrowed as she stared down into her teacup. "If I had known all I should have when I became betrothed..."

"You would not have married Mr. Margrave?"

Adele sighed, as if the weight of the world lowered onto her. "I am most fond of my Roger, and always have been. I just expected other things from my life. Things he should let me help him obtain. We ladies are at the mercy of men, sadly enough. You are wise to stay single, Miss Trentham. Most wise indeed."

Seven

"So, what did you find last night, Mary? When I was forced to tidy and dress myself! What kind of lady's maid are you?" Flora teased as Mary pinned up her red curls in the morning light. She did try to sound stern, but giggled instead at the thought of Mary as a 'proper' lady's maid. She'd be no better at that than was at being a lady's companion.

"You did all right for yourself," Mary said with a sharp poke of a hairpin. "And I had a nice chin-wag with the housemaids. You always say the servants are the ones who know what's what in a big house."

"Very true." And it was. The servants were always there, listening and watching and never speaking, a part of the furniture. Of course they knew the secrets. "What did they say?"

Mary shook her head. "A proper run lot the family is here at Windermere Abbey. Always quarreling and trying to outdo each other. And Lord Windermere— he's always trying to mold his poor daughters into whatever he wants, even though he was no better than he should be in his younger days. I'd say they'd all have an inclination for stealing letters. Or writing them." She lowered her voice and whispered, "Lady Belle might be loudly proclaiming she wants her husband's attention back, but she's been going about with someone else. Not sure who, but give those maids another day or so and they'll have the whole story. One of them told me about some tunnels that run underneath the house and some of the grounds. Excellent places for spying, I'd say."

"Fascinating," Flora said. "Any idea where someone would have stashed the letters if they had them?"

Mary finished Flora's hair, frowning at the plain, tight twist of a style. "Tsk. No flower or ribbon at all. Well, I had a little nose around some of the chambers while you all were at dinner. Adele Margrave has a fancy for bright purple underthings, you'd never have thought it. No sign of anything hidden, but then again these people might be barmy, but they don't really sound stupid. They wouldn't just leave them lying about, and none of their trunks and cases had hidden panels or anything like that."

"True. Strange they might be, but not dim." Flora picked up Chou Chou and cuddled her close, wishing they could send the doggie into chambers to have a *real* nose around. "Plus, I think I've been very silly, assuming someone wanted the letters to use as blackmail. No one's contacted Imogen with demands yet. It could easily be to hide the secret, in which case the letters must be long gone. The duke's ghost doesn't seem to think so, though."

"Look to the father's face," Mary quoted in the duke's booming tone.

"Just so. I looked at every bloomin' man's face until I was cross-eyed over the dinner table! They aren't much to look at, and I couldn't decipher anything."

"Could the old duke be deliberately steering us wrong? Maybe old Margrave put him up to it at the celestial bridge tournament."

Flora considered this as she straightened Chou Chou's bows. "He's annoying, to be sure, but honest. I doubt he'd be interested enough in the matter to bother steering us wrong, anyway. It's not like his own silly diamonds."

"Maybe he was once one of Lady Imogen's lovers!"

Flora laughed, trying to picture the cross old duke, who had shockingly once been in love with a circus dancer, with the fiery, independent Imogen. She would have crushed him beneath her high-heeled slipper, and he wouldn't have stood for that. "Her own brother-in-law and a no-fun-nik like him? I just wish he'd given us more information altogether. What other use would being dead have? What exactly am I supposed to see in this mysterious face?" She put Chou Chou down, and glanced in the mirror to make sure she looked suitably unobtrusive. Maybe she should have brought a pair of spectacles. "Did you find anything at all in your search?"

Mary shook her head as she smoothed and folded away Flora's dinner gown. "Could be in one of the locked jewel-cases Lady Belle, Mrs. Annis, and Adele Margrave have on their dressing tables. No sign anywhere else. There are so many chambers here, though! I could only cover the one corridor."

"Three hundred and eighty seven rooms," Flora murmured, thinking of something Mrs. Appleton the housekeeper mentioned.

Mary snorted. "Who needs that many? Just more to dust."

"And I'm sure they have at least one housemaid to every room to see to that! Too bad we can't recruit all of them as spies." She stood up to make sure the pleated skirt of her pale gray frock was straight. "How do I look, then?"

Mary examined her with pursed lips. "Proper boring."

Flora sighed, and checked the white cuffs edged with a tiny hem of lace. "I can't wait to be home, and in my own clothes again! Tell me what's happening today, again?"

Mary glanced at the schedule left at their door early that morning. "Breakfast. Croquet and tea on the lawn. Bridge. The old duke would like that. Dinner and games."

"Sounds like a good chance for a nose around the gardens." Flora made sure Chou Chou was ensconced on the bed, safe from mischief, and that her sturdy boots were laced up. Hideous they might be, but surely good for trekking around Windermere's vast grounds.

But halfway down the stairs, headed toward the lovely, beckoning smells of breakfast in the dining room, she found herself cornered by Sir Anthony, who seemed to leap out at her from a statuary niche despite his great age.

Flora backed away, wrinkling her nose at his aroma of cigar smoke. She couldn't fathom what Imogen would have seen in him even for a moment. "Sir Anthony. I..."

"I must say, Imogen certainly knows how to choose her employees," he said, leaning even closer with a long wink. Flora was deeply, deeply tired of such men, and had to curl her hands into fists to keep from shoving him down the stairs. They would never find the letters that way. "Tell me, my girl, how long have you worked for her?"

"Long enough to hear plenty of tales of Lady Imogen's very old acquaintances." Flora tried to sound stern but careless. It was trickier than it seemed.

"I do hope she has often spoken of me! What grand times we once had."

Flora tilted her head as if dubious, trying to remember. "No. No, Sir Anthony, I fear your name has not rung any bells."

He reached out like a striking snake and curled his hand tightly around her arm. "I vowed to her once that she'll be sorry for her treatment of me. She has never known a man who could have been more devoted to her, if she could have found kindness in her heart."

Flora, good and angry now, yanked her arm free and tried to slip around him. She wondered if he'd been affronted enough by Imogen's rejection to steal those letters, avenging himself on all those other suitors.

"Sir Anthony. Such tiresome swells of temper so early in the morning, it's quite wearying," a soft, amused voice said. There was a silken swish of skirts on the stairs, and Flora and Sir Anthony glanced back to see Jane Annis floating toward them. She was even more beautiful up close, with skin like peaches in the snow, her dark hair glossy. She seemed cool and unaffected and careless. Flora found she could hardly blame Peter for falling for her.

"Jane," Sir Anthony said, scowling. "You are an early riser today."

"The one thing that can be relied upon at Windermere Abbey is a fine meal. I would hate to miss it," Jane said cheerfully. "You do look as if you could use a hearty feed-up, Sir Anthony, and possibly copious amounts of coffee. Food does seem to improve one's temper wonderfully."

With a huff, he spun around and marched away down the stairs. Flora drew in a clear breath at last, and smiled at Jane.

"Thank you, Mrs. Annis. He was becoming rather a nuisance."

"Oh, I perfectly understand, Miss Trentham. It is always thus with these old gentlemen when Lady Imogen appears. Sir Anthony and Lord Windermere are like dogs with a delectable bone between them; her spell seems long. Peter says she's always had such a fascination about her. So interesting, is it not?" To Flora's surprise, Jane took her arm and walked with her toward the dining room, quite as if they were old bosom bows.

Flora examined the graceful turn of Jane's throat, the soft smile on her rose-pink lips. "You must understand something of what that's like."

Jane laughed merrily. "It is true I have had one or two admirers since my poor husband died, but they all know I am in love now and won't look at anyone else." Her smile faded into a sad little tilt, and she shook her head. "It has been impossible to hide. Such a misfortune."

"Has it been a misfortune? Surely true love is a gift." Not that Flora would know.

Jane tilted her head thoughtfully. "Yes and no, of course. I quite enjoyed my quiet life after I lost my husband. I wasn't looking for romance, let alone one with such drama about it. But when I met Peter—I knew as soon as I looked into his eyes, we were meant to be together. *Had* to be together, if there was any chance of happiness in this life."

Flora thought Jane was quite good at the *drama*, really. Everyone at Windermere was. "Despite the scandal?"

"Peter does not care for such turmoil, either. We would both like to be left alone in the country. He and Belle were already living apart when we met. She didn't care about that, didn't care about Peter, as long as she was a countess. She wanted to live in Town, with parties and friends, not on the estate. If they officially parted..."

Then Belle would not be the countess any longer. She wanted the position; Peter did not. Surely that meant either of them could use the letters for their own ends. "No fury like a woman scorned."

Jane frowned. "She scorned Peter and his needs first! He is such a sensitive soul, so kind and with such a soft heart, it makes the world so difficult for him sometimes. And so many expectations piled on him because of the blasted title. It is fortunate he has me to protect him now."

Flora nodded. She wondered how far Jane would go in her "protection."

"I know you do understand, Miss Trentham. I can tell you also have a sensitive heart," Jane said as they approached the dining room doors, flanked by liveried footmen even so early in the morning. "You are so sympathetic. Perhaps it's your spirit medium gifts. I, too, often sense the presence of the unseen. Perhaps you could speak to Lady Imogen on behalf of Peter, beg for her help? She is his godmother, after all. Peter needs all the friends he can find now."

With one more sweet smile to Flora, Jane glided across the room to sit down next to her beloved, who stared up at her as if she dragged the very sun with her. Adele and Roger sat at the other end of the table, arguing in low, fierce voices. How people loved to squabble there at Windermere! It made Flora quite long for her own peaceful little sitting room. Belle and Lord Winderemre were not there yet, and Sir Anthony was blessedly buried in the newspaper.

Marianne waved at Flora, gesturing to the empty chair beside her. "Miss Trentham, oh do sit next to me! Where is your darling doggie today?"

～

If Flora were able to paint a picture (and she really couldn't even sketch a stick figure), she'd love to put the scene in front of her into watercolors and call it "English Summer Afternoon." The grand house as backdrop, a bright green lawn with figures in pale pinks and blues and creams playing at croquet, flowers scenting the breeze. There didn't even seem the tiniest cloud of turmoil underneath it all.

She studied it from the wicker chair where she sat on the edge of the lawn, which rolled away from her in a sea of soft emerald green toward the house. The hundreds of windows gleamed and glinted in the light like a box of topaz jewels, watching benevolently its unchanging, perfect-seeming world as Henton led a parade of staff to lay out tea-tables with pitchers of lemonade and trays of cakes and sandwiches. Chou Chou watched them from Flora's lap with great interest.

Roger, Adele, Belle, and Benedict played at croquet, their mallets smacking into the balls and sending them flying through wickets. Belle laughed and clapped and hopped about in froths of pink silk and Brussels lace, as if completely unaware of her estranged husband and his mistress sitting in the shade. Adele seemed to be berating Roger for some misplaced shot with his croquet mallet, her finger wagging in his face. He nodded, smiling vaguely from the shadow of his straw hat. Flora had the sense he didn't even hear his wife's words at all.

Benedict waved at Flora, giving her a grimacing half-smile before he turned back to the game. She wondered what he had discovered, or if he was enjoying himself in his courtship of Lady Marianne.

She glanced about for Marianne, and glimpsed her trailing behind her father and Lady Imogen where they took a turn about the edge of the croquet lawn. Marianne held a book in front of her, frowning in concentration at the pages, though Flora wondered how easy it could really be to read while walking and not fall over. It seemed Marianne had much practice at being two places at once—and her book was sideways. Though maybe pretending to read was far preferable to listening to Lord Windermere and Imogen, who seemed to be arguing about something. His arms were crossed over his chest, his head shaking so hard the tassel on his yellow silk cap trembled, and Imogen scowled.

Sir Anthony sat smoking on the terrace, watching them as his old jealousies smoldered like the cigar in his hand.

Benedict abandoned the half-hearted croquet game,

and went to take up a crystal lemonade goblet from the table. He grabbed a second, and came to Flora's side. He handed her one, and flopped down on the grass beside her, looking adorable rumpled in his pale suit, his gold hair tangled over his brow.

"Found anything?" he asked quietly as they watched the scene before them.

Flora told him what Mary did the night before, the chambers and locked jewel-cases, the maids' tales of tunnels under the house. "An excellent hiding place, I'd say. What about you? Anything interesting?"

Benedict grimaced. "Not nearly, I'm afraid. We'll have to get back to the boathouse and take a look at those crates."

Flora nodded. "I admit I never met a hidden box I wasn't dying to open."

He smiled up at her, teasing and radiant. Her heart stuttered just a bit to see it, and she turned away. "Pandora."

She laughed. "I know! I shouldn't. Curiosity and the cat and all. But there it is. We need to find time to look at them, yes. And glance about the attics."

"Tonight, after dinner? I think I heard there were games to be organized."

"Charades?" Flora asked, rather hopefully. She'd not quite left every bit of the stage life behind her, and she adored a bit of playacting beyond being the mousy lady's companion. Not that anyone would invite such a mere companion to play.

"We should hope for something a bit less—visible if we want to sneak away for a good search. And no one wants to see me fumble my way through a round of charades, believe me. Painfully dull and cringe-worthy."

Flora had to disagree. The thought of him stalking about in a scene from, say, *Hamlet*, all clad in black and tormented, was tempting. "Your aunt seems to be spending much time with Lord Windermere today."

She nodded at where Imogen and Windermere now sat in the shade near Jane and Peter, watching the croquet game stagger onward.

"Or perhaps she's avoiding Sir Anthony. He still does seem unhappy she threw him over all those years ago. And he also doesn't seem the sort of man who would stand for being thwarted, even if it takes him eons to remedy it." They studied Sir Anthony as he tossed away his smoke and lit another, glaring at Imogen all the while. "He reminds me of my grandfather. Do you think he'd still be angry enough to steal those letters, if he got an inkling about their existence?"

"Possibly. It seems odd he would hold back from flaunting them in your aunt's face, but maybe he has some sort of longer plan."

"Lord Windermere also seems to harbor an old pash for Aunt Imogen. Look at how he wants to hold her hand even now!" They observed as Lord Windermere tried to sneak out a hand to touch Imogen's only for her to draw back with a glare. "Maybe we're looking at a *crime* here, not blackmail or revenge."

"Possibly. It doesn't matter the age, the heart wants what it wants. What of the estranged Lady Margrave? I haven't had the chance to speak much with Belle. Is she still in love with her husband?" They watched Belle toss down her mallet, and shake back her loosened hair in front of Peter before she marched away.

"From what I've heard, she and Peter were never very fond of each other. Her father arranged the match in her first Season. She enjoys parties and dances, while Peter would rather stay on his estate. Farming and visiting tenants with the beauteous Mrs. Annis."

"It does sound like they were rather unsuited. And Peter and Jane seem happy together." Flora almost sighed at the sight of the lovebirds leaning their heads together, whispering as if the rest of the world wasn't even there. "But being a countess is nothing to sneeze at.

Maybe Belle would go to great lengths to hold that title, if not the man."

"And maybe the man wants to be seen as more than his title," Benedict said softly. Flora had the sense he didn't think only of Peter in those words.

"Not everyone sees position as the be-all, end-all," Flora said, trying so hard not to reach out and touch him, reassure him. "I would guess Peter and his Jane don't. I did ponder whether one of them took the letters to wiggle out of the earldom. If they're going to cause a scandal with a divorce anyway..."

Benedict nodded. "Might as well go off and have a peaceful life. Can't say I would blame them."

Flora saw Lord Windermere turn to his daughter with an irritated glare, and wave Marianne into Benedict's direction. She slowly closed her book and strolled across the lawn. She frowned and dragged her kid half-boots until she saw Chou Chou, and her eyes lit like a bonfire night.

"Your Grace," she said. "And Miss Trentham, and dear Chou Chou! I was hoping I would see you today. Er, all of you, of course. Papa decrees I am not being properly sociable and I should come speak to you, but I should hate to interrupt your conversation." She glanced between them, her brow raised, a smile tugging at the corner of her lips, and Flora had the uncomfortable suspicions Marianne was more perceptive than she appeared.

"Not at all," Benedict said, jumping to his feet to drag another chair into their shade. "Do join us, please. We were just talking about your father's excellent menus here at Windermere, I can't remember when I last ate so well. Shall I fetch you a glass of lemonade, maybe some cake?"

"That would be very welcome on such a warm day, thank you, Your Grace." Marianne reached out to pat Chou Chou, watching as Benedict loped away toward the tea tables, all loose-limbed grace and sunny golden glow. "He is nicer than I expected."

Nice. It wasn't quite what Flora thought when she considered Benedict, but yes indeed, he was a nice person. Funny, easy-going, considerate. It was a rare and underrated quality, and surely one that would make a fine husband, dukie or not. "What did you expect?"

"Oh, the usual sort of thing one sees with such rare beings as dukes. Demanding, short-tempered. Everyone knows that he is younger and more handsome than what you might expect, but I had never heard he was so —so comfortable to be near. Polite. He actually *sees* other people, not just himself."

"That is unusual for all men, not just dukes," Flora muttered.

Marianne laughed. "I fear you are quite right. That's why I have vowed never to marry."

Flora stared at her in surprise. Marianne looked quite decided, her chin raised in defiance. "Never marry?"

Marianne reached for Chou Chou, who happily clambered onto her lap. "I have too much work to do to listen to a man's blather all day. I have been corresponding with Signor Lucelli, a renowned astronomer in Florence, and he thinks my experiments have much merit. I should develop them, and that takes concentration."

"What does your father think of that?"

"I haven't told him," Marianne said with a secret little laugh. Chou Chou licked her chin, making her laugh even more. Flora had the distinct sense that laughing was not something Marianne did on the regular. "But there won't be much he can say! I have an inheritance coming soon from my mother's family, I can take that and get a little cottage somewhere, in the Peak District maybe, where there would be much scope for astronomical observances. He got Belle married off, and look how that went." She gestured at her sister, who sat across the lawn from Peter with her back turned, laughing loudly with Roger and Adele.

"Was your sister never happy, then?"

Marianne seemed to ponder this, watching Belle as she patted Chou Chou's little ears. "Not since she married, no. But then, I'm not sure Belle could ever truly be happy, not for long. She's too much like our father, always thinking something different will make her content and becoming bitter when it isn't what they expected. I think I will stay as I am, no husband at all."

"I'm never one to dissuade people from the single life. It's worked well for me," Flora said. "But I am not a fine lady born. Could you not work *and* be married?"

"Not in the way I want to be. I must focus on one or the other to be good at either." She tilted her head as she watched Benedict chat with Henton over the tea-table, casual and easy and laughing. "Everton *is* nicer than the usual man, but I fear he would not understand me. And surely he deserves far better than a strange girl like me. Papa will just have to get over his disappointment at not having a duchess daughter."

As would Lady Imogen, who had so wanted Benedict to marry Marianne. "Will you not be a bit lonely?"

Marianne studied Flora over Chou Chou's fizzy head, almost making her squirm to be seen so. "Are *you* lonely, Miss Trentham? You are an unmarried, working lady."

"Sometimes I am, yes." Flora did not like to think about that too deeply. She had her work, her friends, and sometimes a lark like this one. She didn't need more. But sometimes, just sometimes, the nights were so very quiet...

"Well, I think I shall be lonely sometimes, as well. But I have my scientific friends whom I correspond with often, and I know I shall meet more." She smiled shyly.

"I have not often had friends. Though once, Belle was my great friend."

Flora had a difficult time picturing such a friendship, even between sisters. Belle was so changeable, so temperamental, Marianne so steady and quiet and studious. Yet Marianne did look so wistful when she said that, so lost in hazy memories that she seemed to lose her grounding and float up into the sky for an instant. Flora's heart ached for her. She patted Marianne's hand as Chou Chou licked her chin again, making her laugh.

"I never had a sister. Not a blood sister, anyway," Flora said. She had Mary and Evie, and lots of girls she'd met in the Follies days. They always had her back, made her laugh. She knew how it would sting to lose them. "What was it like?"

Marianne sniffed, as if to hold back tears, and smiled wider as old pictures crowded around her. "Oh, lovely! She played games with me, taught me piano, sang songs. She listened to me back then. I was always so lonely, you see. Papa was gone so often, and not terribly interested in us when he was here, and our mother died when I was tiny. Cook kept saying we would have a beautiful stepmother, but we never did." She glanced at her father and Lady Imogen, who seemed to have made up whatever they were arguing over and now laughed as if a storm had passed.

"Should you have liked to have a step-mama like Lady Imogen?" Flora asked doubtfully. "She is a wonderful employer, an adventurous, amusing spirit, but as a cozy mama..."

Marianne laughed, even louder when Chou Chou nipped at her nose. "Probably not. She'd always have been running off to London for parties. I had a stupendous governess, Miss Meecham, who saw how much I loved our scientific studies and encouraged me. But I knew no other girls my age, and Belle was such fun. She made everything so much brighter, lighter. Then..."

76

"Then?" Flora said, though she feared she knew what. It was like a play. The bright-sunny, merry girl who found that her husband didn't care for her, and her world darkened, taking everyone else with it.

Marianne shrugged. "We grew up, I suppose, and she couldn't understand me anymore. She made her debut, and started to only think of gowns and dances. And she got married, and I couldn't bear to see how it went so wrong with her. How she should not have followed my father's wishes in her match." She smiled down at Chou Chou, who blinked back. "I do so miss how it used to be for us."

~

The boathouse did not improve its appearance in the daylight. It was still dusty and sagging. Flora knelt beside one of the rotting trunks they glimpsed before, digging through its jumbled contents, but she wasn't very confident of finding anything interesting. Moldy sailcloth, papers so waterlogged she couldn't read them, an old wooden swing seat. "What do you have over there?" she asked Benedict.

He held up a book with a stained leather cover. "*The Romance of the Sea*. A great bestseller twenty years ago, I think."

"It seems odd that this place is so ramshackle when the rest of the Abbey is ready for its own fairytale." A shower of dust dropped from the raw boards of the ceiling, landing in her hair and making her cough. "See what I mean? Not safe even for storage, I would think."

"But no one would look here, if you wanted to keep something secret. Maybe that's the point of it." He held up a frock coat a few decades out of style. "Marianne said she and her sister sometimes picnicked at the pond when they were younger, and there's good fishing there.

77

So I suppose this place isn't a secret, just not much noticed."

Flora dug deeper through the trunk, hoping for a false bottom or hidden compartment. "Marianne seems rather nice."

"Hmm, yes, she is." Benedict seemed distracted by whatever he was examining in an old valise. "More than I expected."

"And scholarly. I'm sure that gives you a lot to talk about over the dining table."

"Probably so. More than most young ladies my aunt seems to like for me, they only know a bit of music and lots about hats. Strange for a woman like Imogen." He shook out another coat and sneezed at the cloud that rose up from the rotting folds of silk. "She doesn't seem very interested in duchess-ing, though. And who could blame her? It's a lot of blasted hard work, especially when an estate needs as much care as mine. Aunt Imogen will just have to keep looking when it comes to my marital prospects. Now, if it was her *own* prospects, I'm sure she would have a great deal more luck."

Flora laughed, thinking of Lord Windermere and Sir Anthony. "She does seem most sought-after by her old suitors. They could never forget her! What were she and Lord Windermere arguing about at croquet?"

Benedict left his now-empty valise and knelt beside Flora to glance in the trunk. He leaned close, smelling of lemons and sunshine in that musty old room. She took a deep breath of him, then wished she didn't when he made her quite dizzy. "Peter and Belle, from what I could hear. Lord Windermere wants them to reconcile, but I think Aunt Imogen wants Peter to stay with Jane and be happy."

"Despite the scandal?"

"Aunt Imogen always slipped off scandal so easily herself, I'm sure she thinks she can do the same for Peter." He read through a sheaf of papers and discarded them when they didn't prove to be interesting.

"I did wonder of Peter and Jane might be looking for a way out of the title."

Benedict frowned in thought. "You think they would use the letters to get some peace and quiet?"

"Maybe."

"Well, who could blame them. Titles are a nuisance. Peter doesn't seem to know about his real parentage, though."

"It's hard to tell *what* he knows, he's so quiet and seems so watchful. Jane told me he is very sensitive and kind when I saw her this morning, though. Unlike Adele, I think she just loves her mate for who he is, not his actual possessions."

Benedict's lips quirked at the corner, as if wistful at such a thought. "Lucky man indeed."

Flora reached out to touch his hand, and pulled back at the last second, curling her fingers into a fist. He didn't need her to tell him what an extraordinary man he was! If he let them, ladies would be tossing themselves at his feet and Imogen would have to find another project than matchmaking. "You could find just the same, dukie, I'm sure."

He tilted his head as he watched her. "How can a duke possibly ever know a lady's true thoughts and feelings?"

"But you are more than that! You are..." He was quite the loveliest man Flora ever met. Not just his sea-eyes and bright hair, that tiny dimple in his chin, but *him*. His laugh, his thoughtfulness, his gentle, humorous ways.

His eyes narrowed. "I am—what?"

"You are..." He was perfect. That was all. "You are—Benedict."

His eyes narrowed, seeming to glow from within with an emerald fire. He leaned closer, closer, so close his warmth wrapped all around her, erasing anything else but him. She forgot herself, forgot their errand, forgot who he really was, and leaned toward him in return, swaying against him as if she couldn't help it. His head bent towards hers, closer, closer...

This was the duke! Her mind seemed to scream it at her. He was not just a man, handsome and tempting, but a duke. They shouldn't do this. Flora knew if she did kiss him, it would mean tumbling down into trouble she certainly did not need.

Flora turned away, flustered and blushing in a way that had never been like her at all. Who had time to get all twirly-minded over a gentleman? But Benedict always brought out such silliness in her. She smoothed her dust-flecked hair, braided back in that plain, stern style that was also not like her, and pasted on a bright, careless smile.

"I think the ghosties are trying to tell us something," she said, and waved at the open trunk.

His cheeks also turned rather pinkish, stained over his cut-glass cheekbones, and he looked away with a rough laugh. "I—yes. We should definitely oblige them by looking. The last thing we want is to make my grandfather angry again."

Flora dug out another thick sheaf of papers, tied together with a bit of twine. "Looks like house plans," she said, holding out one sketch of the front view of the newest wing of the Abbey. "And a map of the grounds."

"What is this?" he said. He turned the map the other way up, and frowned at the squiggly, penciled lines that ran between the rose garden and the lawn, past the outline of the house itself. "These seem to go straight through the Abbey, especially right here at this end where it they widen out."

Flora studied the image for a moment. "Oh, I see! Remember those tunnels we heard about? Maybe that's what those lines are. Surely they're for storage and transport, but where better to hide things. I do think..."

A loud banging sound from outside startled her, and the lid of the trunk slammed. "I think we should get back to the party," Benedict said. "Shall we search those tunnels tonight?"

Flora was quite sure she shouldn't be alone with him in any dark tunnels, but she'd never really been a girl who could resist a dare. She nodded, excitement fluttering inside of her all the way down to her toes in her terrible mud-brown boots. "Yes. Tonight."

Eight

"Five, four, three, two—run!" Peter called, and the party scattered from the sitting room into the corridors beyond. When Adele proposed a game of hide-and-go-seek after dinner, it had been greeted with much enthusiasm. Surely anything, especially finding quiet corners to creep into, had to be better than tensely staring at one another as Belle sniped at Peter, Sir Anthony sniped at Lord Windermere, and Imogen played endless games of Patience on the card table.

It also seemed like the perfect cover for surreptitious searching.

Flora waited in the concealing shadow of a window drapery until she saw Benedict in the corridor, looking about as if he were confused by the running footsteps, the whispers.

"Psst! Dukie, here I am," she hissed. He turned to her with a smile, and held out his hand to her. They ran for the library, hoping no one saw them there.

Windermere's library was enormous, like everything at the Abbey, a long chamber that seemed larger with the vaulted, painted ceiling overhead, a row of window embrasures concealed by velvet draperies, and endless glass-fronted bookcases. A few settees and armchairs were dotted about on the dark green carpet, and one leather-upholstered chaise set beneath the portrait of glowering man in military uniform. The gilt plate on the frame proclaimed him the current Lord Windermere's father, and he did not look best pleased by the goings-on in his home.

A large, blackened steel safe lurked behind a mahogany desk, half-hidden by a potted palm, inviting and forbidding in equal measure in the shadows.

Flora knelt down and carefully studied the mechanism. "A lock-bolt," she murmured. "Easy-peasy." She reached for one of the long pins in her hair. It was not quite like the others that held her braids in place, sharper at one end. She carefully slid it into the mechanism and leaned close to listen to the clicks as she moved it.

"You know how to pick locks?" Benedict said. "Oh, what am I saying—of course you do."

Flora grinned up at him. "A lady must have accomplishments. You never know what this might come in useful."

She heard the telltale "snick" and realized she was on the right track. A few more deft turns, a twist another way, and she had the heavy iron door open. They quickly sorted through the contents—jewel boxes, bills, documents. Letters, but none from Lady Imogen or Lord Margrave.

Flora huffed with disappointment. "You'd think he'd have *something* interesting to look at after all this trouble."

A laugh suddenly sounded outside the library door, high and giddy, and getting louder and closer. Flora carefully shut the safe, and Benedict helped her to her feet and pulled her into a window embrasure, hidden from the room by a drape of gold velvet. Flora peeked between the fabric, trying to see what was so funny.

The door fell open and a couple tumbled into the

room, desperately clinging to each other, kissing, grasping. A few murmured endearments, "pooky darling," "my loveliest pink carnation," floated to Flora's hiding place, and she stifled a giggle in Benedict's satin jacket lapel. She felt an answering laugh rumble through him, deep and rich and warm, quickly cut off. They held onto each other as the couple outside fell to a cushioned chaise with a loud squeak of old springs.

"I've missed this so much!" the lady cried. "Oh, don't stop, my strong old bear-kins!"

Flora peeked past the drapery again, and stifled a startled gasp. It was Belle, and Roger Margrave! He'd obviously escaped his wife's clutches, and *how*. They rolled and grabbed and moaned until Roger fell to the floor. He quickly leaped up and back into Belle's waiting arms.

Flora glanced up at Benedict, and he stared down at her in answering surprise. She was suddenly very aware they, too, embraced in the darkness, but she couldn't make herself move away. Not quite yet.

He leaned sideways against the paneled wall, and it slid a bit under his weight. A gust of stale air escaped. "Look," he mouthed at Flora, gesturing at the surprise doorway. It seemed they had found the entrance to one of those tunnels. Flora nodded, and they slipped inside, leaving the lovebirds on their own.

The air smelled musty there, damp and earthy, and something seemed to echo around them like a cold wind. Flora fumbled in her tapestry bag, which everyone assumed contained a spinster companion's knitting, and found the candles and flint she'd tucked there, along with extra hairpins and a small pistol.

"Of course you have lights," Benedict said, his words catching and bouncing back on the stone walls. "And lock-picks."

"I told you, dukie. You have to be prepared." She caught the wick on one of the candles. It flickered in the cold breeze, but didn't go out, She held it up higher to examine their surroundings, stone walls lined with crates, stretching into the dark distance. She sighed, thinking of how it would take years to search them all. She pulled out the map from the boathouse. "Now, which way do you think we should go next?"

"This way," Benedict said, and tugged her to the right. She had the distinct feeling he was as lost as she was, but she went anyway. They hurried along darkened corridors, right, left, right again, past stacks of crates. When she peeked inside a few, she found they contained mostly tableware, dishes and pans and linens, and strangely, a container of dozens of wigs. But no papers.

After what seemed like hours, they finally went up a short flight of stone steps to find a door to the outside. The iron grille in the door was covered with ivy, but a bit of fresh air leaked past. Benedict put his shoulder against the squeaking portal to shove it open, and they found themselves in the middle of the family burial plot outside the chapel.

Flora froze for a moment, studying the eerie scene. It was like something in a penny dreadful come to life, a moon muffled by clouds gleaming down on the crooked stones and looming mausoleum. An owl cried out in the distance.

"Do you think the ghost monks will descend on us at any moment?" she whispered. She blew out the candle just in case they were attracted by its glow.

Even Benedict looked a bit unsure. "Let's hope not. Come on, maybe we should look in the chapel while we're here." He took her hand and they started down the main pathway, the gravel shining silver in the moonlight. Shadows seemed to flitter and flicker between the stones.

They didn't get as far as the chapel. A ray of that moon fell onto the central pyramid, the tallest of the grave markers, which Mrs. Appleton had said belonged to the last Lord Windermere, the current lord's father. Flora studied it carefully. *Your smile has gone forever, Father, and your hand we cannot touch, but you are with us always.* Below that truly terrible little verse was a bas relief carving of a man glaring out at them. That didn't look like a smile to be much missed.

But there was something about it...

"Look, dukie!" she exclaimed, gesturing to the etchings. "It's the father's face."

Benedict stared at the pyramid in astonishment, before he laughed and squeezed her hand. "So it is! How clever you are, Flora. Do you think we're supposed to—dig here or something?"

Flora shuddered at the thought. "I hope not. It must be awfully cold and clammy." She glanced around, at the teahouse on the hilltop, the chimneys of the Abbey. Light gleamed on a flash of glass at one of the windows of Marianne's tower. It seemed to be focused right on the pyramid.

"Maybe we could start there," she said. Hopefully no grave robbing would be necessary quite yet.

Nine

Marianne's tower didn't look like anything a human being should venture inside, let alone work on scientific experiments in there. It seemed to lean decidedly to one side, the bricks about to tumble away. There was no front door, but an opening that led through piles of old leaves to a spiral staircase. Most of the windows were tangled over with ivy, but enough light crept in that Flora could see dirt-streaked white tile walls, a broken flagstone floor.

There was no place to hide anything there. They would have to go up those stairs.

Flora glanced back at Benedict, who stared thoughtfully up into the darkness above those stairs. Did the old railings actually *sway*? Would it come away from the wall at any moment? Only one way to find out. Flora hefted her bag higher in her arms and started climbing.

The stairs creaked under her boots, but they didn't give way. The tower was sturdier than it looked, staying firm as they climbed past narrow windows.

At the top was large, circular room surrounded on all sides by more windows. In the daytime, surely the whole estate could be kept under surveillance there. There were books piled everywhere, falling of shelves and stacked against the brick wall, and long tables scattered with mysterious equipment and notebooks.

One of the windows boasted a most expensive-looking large telescope, which seemed to be what had gleamed as it focused down on the burial plot. Its mirrored face lay on its side nearby, and standing with one arm in the apparatus, the other hand clutching a sheaf of handwritten letters, was—Marianne.

She spun around and gaped at them for a long moment, all three of them frozen in shock. Her pale blue evening gown fluttered in the wind from an open window, and her hand trembled. Her stare flickered desperately to the doorway, but Benedict and Flora still stood there, and it was clear there was no escape. She slumped down onto a nearby bench, the papers clutched against her waist.

"You found me," she said softly. "Papa will be angry I left the party."

"Who cares about that?" Flora cried. "Are those Lady Imogen's letters?"

Marianne stared up at them in wide-eyed astonishment. "How do you know about those? Are you—oh. I see." She scowled. "You are not a lady's companion! Are you really a spirit medium? Did a ghost tell you about this?"

"Something like that," Flora answered. "It's true we've been here at the Abbey looking for those. Why do *you* have them?"

"My aunt would very much like them back," Benedict said sternly. "As I'm sure you know, Lady Marianne. Are you intending to blackmail her with them?"

"Blackmail? No!" Marianne held the papers straight out as if they would bite her. "I haven't even read them. I don't know what's in them at all, I swear. I'm just hiding them here for a while."

Flora and Benedict exchanged a long glance. Could they believe her? He grabbed the letters out of

Marianne's grasp and tucked them safely inside his jacket.

"Why did you bother taking them from Imogen's house, then?" he demanded. "And how did you get into her safe?"

"Much the same way we did tonight, I suspect." Flora said, studying the scientific implements, including very sharp tweezers and blades, on one of the tables. Marianne obviously had many hidden depths. She wondered if the lady might enjoy help as a medium's assistant.

"I—I didn't. That is, I looked up some information about picking locks but I never tried it myself," Marianne protested. She seemed on the verge of tears, her slender shoulders trembling, her voice choked. "Belle said it would just..." She gasped, and clamped her mouth shut.

"It was *Belle* who took them?" Flora said, her thoughts flying. It seemed the estranged Lady Belle didn't spend all her time rolling about on library chaises, then.

Marianne buried her face in her hands. "She met someone named—Henry, I think? Harry. He knew about Peter and Jane, you see, and told Belle he could help her take back some control in her marital dilemma. For a price."

"Hidey-Place Harry," Flora growled, with a stamp of her too-sensible boot. "Of course! The weasel. And he must have shown her how to pick a lock."

Marianne nodded. "And told her she should look in Lady Imogen's safe at her party."

"What was she going to do with them?" Benedict asked, his voice gentle now as they saw Marianne wasn't quite to blame in the mess.

"I don't know, I promise I don't. She just said they were like diamonds to her, and asked me to hide them until she decided what to do. I just missed my sister so much! This seemed like a way she would pay attention to me again."

Flora nodded, remembering how wistful Marianne seemed at the croquet game as she talked of her lonely childhood, of her sister's friendship.

"I was just going to keep them for a while, to try and persuade Belle to let me help her." Marianne gave her eyes a furious swipe. "What are you going to do? Are you going to tell my father? He so much wants Lady Imogen to like him again."

Flora and Benedict exchanged another long, speaking glance. "I don't think so. But we are going to take these, Lady Marianne. Tell your sister she must find another way out of her marital troubles." Maybe by eloping with Roger or something.

"Do you have the feeling your betrothal is off?" she whispered to Benedict under Marianne's sobs.

He smiled, a sunburst of light in all the gloom. "Oh, Flora. I do hope so."

Epilogue

" I shall never write another indiscreet letter!" Lady Imogen said as she fed the purloined missives into Flora's sitting room fireplace. She paused, one paper held aloft. "Or rather, I shall never *keep* an indiscreet letter again."

"I shall hold you to that, Aunt Imogen," Benedict answered, kicking his feet up onto a hassock as he sipped at his brandy and watched the fire consume all that trouble. Flora laughed, and cuddled Chou Chou close as Mary passed more brandy.

Imogen tossed in the last letter and dropped down on one of the armchairs with a deep sigh. "A lady must hope for some adventure ahead, or what fun is life?" Mary handed her another drink. "Are you quite sure, my dears, you cannot tell me exactly where you found the dratted things?"

Flora smiled down into her glass, and sensed Benedict doing the same. "It was purely a lucky chance, Lady Imogen, when we stumbled upon them. Or rather, Chou Chou did."

Chou Chou, who had been lolling asleep in her guest bedchamber when Flora and Benedict found the tower, blinked up at them innocently. It was always easy to blame, or credit, the dog.

"Ah, well, I suppose it wouldn't have mattered to Peter one way or the other, really," Imogen said. She seemed quite pensive, almost sad, as she examined the flickering fire, the drifting ashes of her letters. "But I should have certainly hated for there to be any blot on his father's memory for him, no matter what he does in the future."

"And what will Peter do now?" Benedict asked.

"Politics are out for him, alas," Imogen said. "How his father would have hated that! He could have gone so far. I see now he has no fire for the work, though. At least he still has the title. He and Jane Annis will settle at the estate, I imagine."

"And Belle?" Flora asked, wondering if the lady had been *very* furious when she found her stolen letters stolen back again.

"Off to Italy with Marianne, I believe. An extended holiday. I daresay when she returns, we shall soon hear of a divorce petition." Her lips twisted in a distasteful little moue. "It was not thus in *my* day. Once a decision was made, it had to be stuck to. Though maybe we were quite wrong back then."

"It seems Italy is the popular thing now," Mary said. "I read in the Society pages that Roger Margrave is headed there right now. Adele Margrave is for Brighton, on a sea cure."

Flora and Benedict laughed, as if they both thought of squeaking springs and library trysts. "It should be quite the crowd in Florence or Pisa. I am glad to hear Lady Marianne is accompanying her sister." Maybe it meant they could be friends after all, despite Marianne losing the letters.

Imogen sighed. "Yes, but so very vexing she isn't here to marry Benedict!"

Benedict gave her a rueful smile. "I don't think we would have suited each other, aunt."

"Ah, well. I'm sure there are ever so many young

ladies here in London who would be most eager to make your acquaintance! Or maybe an American heiress. They are becoming rather fashionable, aren't they? And I shall introduce you to every one of them." Lady Imogen looked quite cheerful at the prospect of such vigorous matchmaking, but Benedict gave her a stare filled with alarm. Flora would have laughed if she didn't feel quite so sorry for him.

"Perhaps I shall give a party..." Imogen mused.

"But look at what happened at your last party," he reminded her quickly.

"Hmm. Perhaps you are right, Benedict dear. Once I hire more security and clean out my letter-boxes, we shall have a ball. A bride hunt ball!" Imogen said. "Maybe Chou Chou could help us? She does seem a most clever pup."

Chou Chou sat up in interest until Flora gave her a sharp glance. Surely Benedict could stay single a little while longer.

"Chou Chou has a lot of work to do here," Flora said. "We have ever so many séances on the books now!"

And no real ghosts welcome...

Also by Amanda McCabe

Flora Flowerdew Victorian Mysteries
Flora Flowerdew and the Mystery of the Duke's Diamonds
Flora Flowerdew and the Mystery of the Purloined Papers
Flora Flowerdew and the Secret of the Sarcophagus

Kate Haywood Elizabethan Mysteries
Murder at the Princess' Palace
Murder at Westminster Abbey
Murder in the Queen's Garden
Murder at the Queen's Masquerade
Murder at Whitehall
Murder at the Royal Chateau

Daughters of Erin
Countess of Scandal
Duchess of Sin
Lady of Seduction

Scandalous St. Claires
One Naughty Night
Two Sinful Secrets

Regency Rebels
Because of Miss Everdean
The Earl's Misplaced Bride
Delighting the Duke
The Earl's Second Chance

About the Author

Amanda McCabe wrote her first romance at the age of sixteen--a vast historical epic starring all her friends as the characters, written secretly during algebra class (and her parents wondered why math was not her strongest subject...)

She's never since used algebra, but her books (set in a variety of time periods--Regency, Victorian, Tudor, Renaissance, and 1920s) have been nominated for many awards, including the RITA Award, the Romantic Times BOOKReviews Reviewers' Choice Award, the Booksellers Best, the National Readers Choice Award, and the Holt Medallion. She lives in New Mexico with her lovely husband, along with far too many books and a spoiled rescue dog.

When not writing or reading, she loves yoga, collecting cheesy travel souvenirs, and watching the Food Network--even though she doesn't cook. She also writes as Laurel McKee. historical Elizabethan mysteries as Amanda Carmack., and Eliza Casey...

Please visit her at http://ammandamccabe.com